P9-DGY-532

WHO WILL SURVIVE?

IT'S GOING TO BE A
KILLER
YEAR!

Is the senior class at Shadyside High doomed? That's the prediction Trisha Conrad makes at her summer party—and it looks as if she may be right. Spend a year with the Fear Street seniors, as each book in this new series brings horror after horror.
Will anyone reach graduation day alive?

Only R.L. Stine knows...

Trisha Conrad

LIKES:
Shopping in the mall my dad owns, giving fabulous parties, Gary Fresno

REMEMBERS:
The murder game, the senior table at Pete's Pizza

HATES:
Rich girl jokes, bad karma, overalls

QUOTE:
"What you don't know will hurt you."

Clark Dickson

LIKES:
Debra Lake, poetry, painting

REMEMBERS:
Trisha's party, the first time I saw Debra

HATES:
Nicknames, dentists, garlic pizza, tans

QUOTE:
"Fangs for the memories."

Jennifer Fear

LIKES:
Basketball, antique jewelry, cool music

REMEMBERS:
The doom spell, senior cut day, hanging with Trisha and Josie

HATES:
The way people are afraid of the Fears, pierced eyebrows

QUOTE:
"There's nothing to fear but fear itself."

Jade Feldman

LIKES:
Cheerleading, expensive clothes, working out

REMEMBERS:
Ice cream and gab fests with Dana

HATES:
Cheerleading captains, ghosts, SAT prep courses

QUOTE:
"You get what you pay for."

Gary Fresno

LIKES:
Hanging out by the bleachers, art class, gym

REMEMBERS:
Cruisin' down Division Street with the guys, that special night with that special person (you know who you are...)

HATES:
My beat-up Civic, working after school everyday, cops

QUOTE:
"Don't judge a book by its cover."

Kenny Klein

LIKES:
Jade Feldman, chemistry, Latin, baseball

REMEMBERS:
The first time I beat Marla Newman in a debate, Junior Prom with Jade

HATES:
Nine-year-olds who like to torture camp counselors, cafeteria food

QUOTE:
"Look before you leap."

Debra Lake

LIKES:
Sensitive guys, tennis, Clark's poems

REMEMBERS:
Basketball games, when Clark painted my portrait

HATES:
Possessive boyfriends and jealous girlfriends

QUOTE:
"I would do anything for you, but I won't do that."

Stacy Malcolm

LIKES:
Sports, funky hats, shopping

REMEMBERS:
Running laps with Mary, stuffing our faces at Pete's, Mr. Morley and Rob

HATES:
Psycho killers, stealing boyfriends

QUOTE:
"College, here I come!"

Josh Maxwell

LIKES:
Debra Lake, Debra Lake, Debra Lake

REMEMBERS:
Hanging out at the old mill, senior camp-out, Coach's pep talks

HATES:
Funeral homes, driving my parents' car, tomato juice

QUOTE:
"Sometimes you don't realize the truth until it bites you right on the neck."

Josie Maxwell

LIKES:
Black clothes, black nail polish, black lipstick, photography

REMEMBERS:
Trisha's first senior party, the memorial wall

HATES:
Algebra, evil spirits (including Marla Newman), being compared to my stepbrother Josh

QUOTE:
"The past isn't always the past—sometimes it's the future."

Mickey Myers

LIKES:
Jammin' with the band, partying, hot girls

REMEMBERS:
Swimming in Fear Lake, the storm, my first gig at the Underground

HATES:
Dweebs, studying, girls who diet, station wagons

QUOTE:
"Shadyside High rules!"

Marla Newman

LIKES:
Writing, cool clothes, being a redhead

REMEMBERS:
Yearbook deadlines, competing with Kenny Klein, when Josie put a spell on me (ha ha)

HATES:
Girls who wear all black, guys with long hair, the dark arts

QUOTE:
"The power is divided when the circle is not round."

Mary O'Connor

LIKES:
Running, ripped jeans, hair spray

REMEMBERS:
Not being invited to Trisha's party, rat poison

HATES:
Social studies, rich girls, cliques

QUOTE:
"Just say no."

Dana Palmer

LIKES:
Boys, boys, boys, cheerleading, short skirts

REMEMBERS:
Senior camp-out with Mickey, Homecoming, the back seat

HATES:
Private cheerleading performances, fire batons, sharing clothes

QUOTE:
"The bad twin always wins!"

Deirdre Palmer

LIKES:
Mysterious guys, sharing clothes, old movies

REMEMBERS:
The cabin in the Fear Street woods, sleepovers at Jen's

HATES:
Being a "good girl," sweat socks

QUOTE:
"What you see isn't always what you get."

Will Reynolds

LIKES:
The Turner family, playing guitar, clubbing

REMEMBERS:
The first time Clarissa saw me without my dreads, our booth at Pete's

HATES:
Lite FM, the clinic, lilacs

QUOTE:
"I get knocked down, but I get up again..."

Ty Sullivan

LIKES:
Cheerleaders, waitresses, Fears, psychics, brains, football

REMEMBERS:
The graveyard with you know who, Kenny Klein's lucky shot

HATES:
Painting fences, Valentine's Day

QUOTE:
"The more the merrier."

Clarissa Turner

LIKES:
Art, music, talking on the phone

REMEMBERS:
Shopping with Debra, my first day back to school, eating pizza with Will

HATES:
Mira Block

QUOTE:
"Real friendship never dies."

Matty Winger

LIKES:
Computers, video games, Star Trek

REMEMBERS:
The murder game—good one Trisha

HATES:
People who can't take a joke, finding Clark's cape with Josh

QUOTE:
"Don't worry, be happy."

Phoebe Yamura

LIKES:
Cheerleading, gymnastics, big crowds

REMEMBERS:
That awesome game against Waynesbridge, senior trip, tailgate parties

HATES:
When people don't give it their all, liars, vans

QUOTE:
"Today is the first day of the rest of our lives."

R.L. Stine
Seniors
A FEAR STREET Super Chiller

episode three **The Thirst**

A Parachute Press Book

A GOLD KEY PAPERBACK

Golden Books Publishing Company, Inc.
New York

www.fearstreet.com

A Gold Key Paperback Original

Golden Books Publishing Company, Inc.
888 Seventh Avenue
New York, NY 10106

FEAR STREET and associated characters, slogans and logos are trademarks and/or registered trademarks of Parachute Press, Inc. Based on the FEAR STREET book series by R.L. Stine. All rights reserved, including the right to reproduce this book or portions thereof in any form whatsoever. For information address Golden Books.

Copyright © 1998 by Parachute Press, Inc.

GOLD KEY and design are registered trademarks of Golden Books Publishing Company, Inc.

ISBN: 0-307-24707-4

First Gold Key paperback printing September 1998

10 9 8 7 6 5 4 3 2 1

Photographer: Jimmy Levin

Printed in the U.S.A.

The Thirst

PART ONE

Chapter One

The Body on the Gym Floor

Dana Palmer pulled on a velvety purple top over tight black jeans and checked her reflection in the dresser mirror. A small gold hoop and a red glass stud glinted from each earlobe. Her shoulder-length blond hair gleamed and her eyes sparkled.

First day of school, she thought excitedly. First day of my senior year.

And my last year at Shadyside High.

I can't believe it—it's going to be so great!

As she grabbed a brush and began tugging it through her hair, she heard a loud thump from the closet. "Deirdre, is that you?"

A muffled voice called out something Dana didn't understand. Dana heard another thump, and the sound of wire hangers pinging against each other.

1

Finally Dana's twin sister Deirdre backed out of the closet, carrying an armful of clothes.

Deirdre Palmer had the same good looks—blond hair, the same wide-set eyes, the same pointed chin as her sister.

They appeared nearly identical—except that Deirdre had a tiny mole high on her left cheekbone.

And instead of looking excited about the first day of school, Deirdre had a worried, hassled expression on her face.

"Deirdre, I thought you were downstairs having breakfast already!" Dana pointed the hairbrush at her twin's fuzzy blue bathrobe. "You're not even dressed! What on earth have you been doing?"

Deirdre tossed the clothes onto her bed. "Trying to decide what to wear," she replied with a sigh.

"Now?" Dana couldn't believe it. "We have to leave in ten minutes!"

"I know." Deirdre bit her lip and stared at the jumble of jeans, miniskirts and tops. "I just can't make up my mind." She picked up a short, pleated skirt.

"Whoa—that's mine," Dana warned.

Deirdre dropped it.

"Wear your jeans. Or your leggings," Dana suggested. "And that big red shirt. It's cool."

"Yeah, but it's dirty, and I forgot to put it in the

2

wash." Deirdre picked up a green-and-gray plaid shirt, then tossed it aside. "I want to look really, really good."

"Oh? Who's the guy?" Dana teased.

"Huh? Nobody," Deirdre replied quickly. "It's just because it's the first day of school and everything, that's all."

Dana kept brushing her hair and watching in the mirror as Deirdre finally picked out a straight, black mini-skirt and a pale blue, tank top.

She's lying about the guy, Dana thought, seeing the flush on her sister's cheeks. There's got to be a guy. I wonder who he is.

Fumbling with the zipper, Deirdre zipped up the skirt, then tugged the top over her head. She crossed to the dresser and stood next to Dana. When she stared into the mirror, her shoulders slumped and she sighed again.

"What is the matter with you?" Dana demanded. "You act as if you're going to a funeral or something. Come on, this is our senior year! Aren't you excited?"

"A little."

Deirdre began twisting her hair into a French braid. "But I'm kind of down, too. I mean, high school is almost over and I haven't done anything!"

"What are you talking about?"

"Well, look at *you*," Deirdre said. "You're on the

cheerleading squad, you make good grades, you've had lots of boyfriends."

"So?"

Deirdre sighed again. "So you've done everything you wanted. I need four more years just to figure out who I am!"

Dana stifled a groan. Deirdre thinks too much, that's her problem, she told herself. If she would just loosen up and stop worrying about who she is, she'd have a great time.

A car horn blared loudly from the street.

Dana dropped her brush and raced to the window. "It's Mickey. He's in the driveway," she announced. "Come on, Deirdre, enough already. Stop playing with your hair. Let's go!"

Dana grabbed her book bag and trotted downstairs. She snatched a blueberry muffin from the kitchen counter and hurried to the front door. "Meet you outside, Deirdre!" she called over her shoulder. "And hurry!"

Dana had been going out with Mickey Myers all summer. He sat in his black, souped-up Firebird, tapping his fingers on the steering wheel, revving the motor while he waited.

When he spotted Dana, he stuck his blond head out the driver's window and whistled. "Looking good!"

Dana trotted up and gave him a quick kiss. "You, too," she declared.

She really liked him. He was a great, fun guy.

He drove fast and liked to party, and he didn't take many things very seriously. But she wasn't sure how long it would last. Everyone knew that Mickey Myers had an eye for other girls.

Oh, well, she thought as she ran around the car and climbed into the passenger seat. I can't complain. After all, I like plenty of other guys, too.

Who wants to be tied down? It's much more fun this way.

As Deirdre emerged from the house, Mickey leaned out the window and whistled again.

Startled, Deirdre stumbled on a crack in the sidewalk. She caught her balance, then slipped into the back seat, her cheeks flaming.

What is her problem? Dana wondered.

Mickey revved the motor loudly. "Look out, Shadyside High!" he shouted, leaning on the horn. "Here come the seniors!" He put the car in gear and shot away from the curb in a squeal of rubber.

Deirdre gasped.

Dana laughed. She liked the speed and the feel of the cool wind in her hair.

She broke her blueberry muffin in two and gave Mickey half. He wolfed it down and leaned on the horn again, zipping through the winding streets, heading toward Shadyside High on Park Drive.

"Watch out!" Deirdre cried.

5

Mickey hit the brakes and waited impatiently as a silver Celica backed out of a driveway in front of them. A girl with long, wavy black hair sat behind the wheel. Dana recognized Danielle Cortez, another member of the cheerleader squad, and waved to her.

Danielle braked and leaned her head out the window. "Dana, don't forget—Phoebe called a cheerleader's meeting in the gym, first thing! She said it's important."

"I remember. See you there!" Dana shouted.

Danielle drove off.

Dana leaned back against the seat, frowning. "Why do we have to meet first thing?" she grumbled. "Phoebe is spoiling the first morning. I mean, that's when we get to wander around the halls, and talk, and check everybody out."

"Well, she *is* the head cheerleader," Deirdre pointed out.

"Don't remind me." Dana sighed. Phoebe Yamura had been named head cheerleader at the end of junior year, and Dana couldn't help feeling a little jealous.

"Hey, check it out!" Mickey cried suddenly. He pointed to a car turning into the intersection. "It's Debra Lake. And look who she's with—Count Clarkula!"

Count Clarkula was everybody's private nickname for Clark Dickson. With his black hair and intense dark eyes, Clark reminded people of

6

Dracula. His personality didn't help, either.

For one thing, he almost always wore black. And he spent most of his time painting and writing weird poetry.

"I still can't believe Debra broke up with Josh," Dana said. Josh Maxwell was smart and cute and fun to be with. "I mean, what can she possibly see in Clark Dickson?"

"She has fallen under his spell!" Mickey replied in a menacing vampire voice. "Count Clarkula wants her blood. Watch out, Dana—you will be next!"

Dana turned her attention away from Clark and sat forward excitedly as Mickey turned onto the campus of Shadyside High.

"There's Stacy Malcolm. Hey, Stacy!" Deirdre waved to a tall, long-legged girl striding toward the school.

Stacy, star of the basketball and track teams, took off her hat and waved it. She almost always wore a hat. Today it was a bright yellow baseball cap with an incredibly long bill. Anybody else would have looked like a duck, but Stacy managed to look cool in it.

Mickey finally found a parking spot in the back of the student lot. As the three of them climbed out of the Firebird, Dana saw Danielle Cortez leaving her Celica and hurrying toward the school.

Dana checked her wristwatch. "I'd better run

ahead," she said. "I can't be late. The cheerleader meeting is supposed to start in about three minutes."

"Hey, you forgot something," Mickey told her.

Dana glanced around. "What?" she asked.

Mickey tapped his lips.

With a laugh Dana stood on tiptoe and gave him a kiss. Out of the corner of her eye, she saw Deirdre's face turn pink.

What gives? Dana wondered again. She's seen me kiss plenty of guys.

As she hurried through the parking lot, Dana spotted Debra Lake again, walking with Mira Block. She glanced around for Clark, but he was nowhere in sight.

Clark probably changed into a bat and flew inside, Dana thought with a smile.

"Dana?" a voice called out.

Dana turned and waited for Jade Feldman, another cheerleader, to catch up to her. "I didn't get my locker assignment, so I have to stop by the office," Jade declared. "I might be late for the meeting. Will you tell *Phoebe*?"

"Sure," Dana replied, amused. Jade made Phoebe's name sound like a dirty word. No wonder. Jade tried out for head cheerleader, too. "See you in the gym."

Dana trotted up the steps and pushed through the front doors of the school. Then she threaded her way through the crowded halls, shouting 'hi' and waving to kids she knew.

The crowds had almost disappeared by the time she reached the gym. It stood at the end of a long hall. The only other door led into the band room, which was empty.

Dana pushed open the gym doors and let them clang shut behind her.

The gym was empty and dark.

Weird, she thought. "Hellooo?" Her voice echoed off the high, tile walls. "Phoebe? Anybody?"

Silence.

Scowling, Dana glanced around again, searching for a light switch. Her eye caught something white on the floor at the far end of the bleachers.

Sneakers?

The blob of white took shape as she drew closer. Yes. Definitely hightop sneakers.

And then Dana saw legs. A body. Long, wavy black hair.

Someone wearing the sneakers. Someone sprawled on the gym floor.

Danielle Cortez!

"Danielle!" Dana shrieked. And then she saw a movement across the gym.

A blur of black.

Then a flash of yellow light as someone ran out the side door.

Dana dropped to her knees beside Danielle.

She's so still! Dana thought.

She touched the girl's arm.

And snatched her hand back with a horrified gasp.

So cold.

Cold as death . . .

Chapter Two

A Scream and a Crash

Her whole body shaking with horror, Dana rose to her feet.

Her legs trembled as she began backing away from Danielle's body.

Footsteps!

Coming up fast behind her!

Has Danielle's murderer returned?

With a terrified gasp, she spun around.

Clark Dickson stared back at her. Dressed all in black, he blended into the deep shadows.

Dana's heart thundered against her chest. "Clark—what—what are you doing in here?" she demanded.

"I heard a scream," Clark said softly. "I hurried in—"

"Danielle," Dana whispered. She gestured to the gym floor behind her. "I found her. She's not moving! Clark . . . I . . . I think she's dead!"

"Huh?" Stepping swiftly around Dana, Clark dropped down beside Danielle. He gently brushed his hand across the dead girl's cheek.

"Ohh," he murmured. His eyes flashed as he gazed up at Dana. "She's so pale . . ."

Dana stood in the parking lot later that day. She wrapped her arms around herself to keep from shaking. "I wish Mickey would hurry up," she murmured. "So what if he forgot his backpack? Couldn't he take us home first and then come back and get it later?"

"This is so horrible!" Josie Maxwell cried. She joined Dana, Deirdre, and Trisha Conrad in the parking lot. "I still can't believe it."

"Believe it," Dana muttered. "I found her, remember?"

"I know. I'm sorry," Josie replied quickly. She hugged Dana. "It must have been awful. You must be so upset."

"Yeah." Dana gazed around. Groups of kids huddled together, talking about Danielle. Teachers stood murmuring in small groups, worried expressions on their faces.

Two police cars stood in front of the school, red roof lights flashing. Earlier, there had been five squad cars, plus an ambulance.

The ambulance had left hours ago, carrying Danielle's dead body to the morgue.

Her pale, cold body.

Dana shuddered. From the minute she'd found Danielle, the day had been a nightmare.

Sirens wailing. Kids crying.

An emergency assembly to talk about the murder.

Police everywhere, questioning everybody.

Dana turned to see Matty Winger hurrying toward her. His backpack bounced on his back as he ran.

"Hey, Dana—I heard you found her," Matty said breathlessly. "What did she look like?"

"Matty!" Trisha gasped. "That's a horrible thing to ask. What makes you think Dana wants to talk about it?"

"Matty, she looked like you on a *good* day!" Dana snapped.

Matty rolled his eyes. "Give me a break. You can't blame me for being curious, can you?" He turned back to Dana. "So? What did she look like?"

"Like she was asleep," Dana told him. "Her skin was cold and . . ."

"You *touched* her?" Josie gasped.

Dana rolled her eyes. "I didn't know she was dead—okay? I thought maybe she fainted. Anyway, she was cold and really pale."

"No kidding?" Matty's blue eyes widened. "Real pale?"

"That's what I said," Dana muttered, frowning. "Why?"

"Nothing. It's just weird, that's all." Shaking his head, Matty trotted through the parking lot to his car.

"I have to go," Josie declared. She had a waitress job after school at Pete's Pizza. "I'll call you later, Deirdre."

"Okay. This is so horrible," Deirdre repeated after Josie left. "I mean, who would believe a murder on the first day of school?"

Trisha sighed. "I would."

"Huh?" Dana frowned again. "Trisha—what do you mean?"

"I told you this would happen." Trisha's eyes clouded with worry. "Remember? I had a vision? About our class?"

Dana's frown deepened. "Oh. Right. You pictured us all dead. We're doomed, right? The whole class."

Trisha nodded, a faraway look in her brown eyes. "That's why I'm not surprised about Danielle. I didn't know exactly what would happen. But I knew *some*thing would."

A horn honked close by.

Trisha's eyes suddenly lit up.

Dana turned and saw Gary Fresno driving toward them in his beat-up Civic. He stopped and flung open the passenger door.

Trisha grabbed her backpack and hurried over to him.

"Whoa," Dana murmured. "The last I heard, Gary was going with Mary O'Connor. When did he start seeing Trisha?"

"Since her party at the beginning of summer," Deirdre replied. "Trisha is crazy about him."

14

Dana watched as Gary's car rattled away. What a weird couple. Gary lived in the Old Village, not the nicest part of town. And he hung out with a rough crowd.

Super-rich Trisha Conrad always wore the latest designer clothes and lived in a mansion overlooking the Cononka river. She had a house full of servants. An actual butler even answered the front door.

"Does Mary know about this?" Dana asked.

"Huh?"

Dana scowled at her sister. "Hello? Did you hear anything I've been saying?"

"Not really," Deirdre admitted. "I was thinking about what Trisha said. About her psychic flash."

"What does that have to do with anything?" Dana asked.

She shivered. "What if she's right, Dana? What if our class really is doomed?"

"Whoa. That's crazy," Dana replied quickly. She didn't want to think about it. It was too weird. Too scary. Besides, it couldn't possibly be true.

"It's crazy," she repeated.

"But Trisha has had these flashes all her life," Deirdre reminded her. "And they always come true. Always. Maybe . . ."

A scream interrupted her.

Dana jumped and cried out. The scream sent shivers up her spine.

So shrill.

So full of terror.

Chapter Three

The New Boy

That scream! Deirdre thought. That terrifying scream.

Somebody is hurt—maybe even dead.

Glancing frantically around, she saw a plume of steam rising into the air at the front of the parking lot. Several kids raced toward it, shouting and pointing.

"Come on!" Dana cried. She grabbed her sister's arm and pulled her toward the rising steam.

It's going to be awful, Deirdre thought. I just know it. No one could scream like that and not be hurt.

"Whoa!" Dana stopped suddenly as the accident came into view.

"Oh, wow!" Deirdre gasped.

Gary's Civic—smashed up against the rear of

16

another car. The fenders of both cars crumpled like foil. Shattered tail- and headlight glass littered the ground. Steam hissed from under the Civic's hood.

Deirdre shut her eyes. "Trisha and Gary," she whispered shakily. "Are they . . . ?"

"No big deal," Dana murmured. "It was just a fender-bender. Looks like everyone is okay."

Deirdre opened her eyes. Beyond a group of excited, chattering students, she saw Gary and Trisha. They stood close together, their arms around each other as they stared at the Civic.

"Hey—there's Mickey!" Dana cried, watching him come trotting down the front steps of the school. "Finally! Want a ride, Deirdre?"

"I'm waiting for Jennifer and Stacy," Deirdre told her. "One of them will take me home."

As Dana hurried off, Deirdre heard a muffled cry from behind her. Turning, she saw Mary O'Connor staring at the crash scene.

No—not at the crash, Deirdre realized.

Mary stared at Gary. Holding Trisha so tightly.

Mary didn't notice Deirdre. She didn't seem to see anything but her boyfriend, hugging another girl. Her chin trembled and tears formed in her eyes.

She didn't know! Deirdre realized. Mary didn't know about Gary and Trisha.

Before Deirdre could say anything to her, Mary ran off.

Deirdre turned back to the crash scene. Gary was inspecting the damage now. Trisha leaned against the rear of the Civic, a worried expression on her face.

Deirdre crunched across the broken glass toward her friend. "Trisha! Thank goodness you guys are all right!" she called. "Who was in the other car?"

"Nobody," Trisha replied. "It was just parked there." She sighed. "I screamed when I saw we were going to crash, but Gary couldn't stop in time. His brakes—they just gave out. He pumped and pumped. But . . ."

Trisha glanced at Gary and lowered her voice. "Gary's broke. He knew he needed brakes, but he couldn't afford them. Now this. He's really upset."

"Well, at least you guys are okay," Deirdre told her. "It could be worse."

Much worse, she thought.

Deirdre gave Trisha a hug and then started walking toward the school. Where were Jennifer and Stacy? The day had been a nightmare. Deirdre was desperate to get away.

"Deirdre?" a guy's voice called.

Deirdre turned and saw a lanky guy with thick dark hair striding toward her.

"Deirdre?" he repeated.

"Yes?" I've seen him before, Deirdre thought. Where?

The guy stopped. Long, thick lashes framed

his pale gray eyes. "I thought that was you. Whoa. I just saw somebody who looks exactly like you getting into a car with another guy. Same face, different clothes. Let me guess—you're . . ."

"A twin." Deirdre stared hard at the boy. "You must have seen my sister, Dana." Who is this guy? she wondered.

"I'm Jon Milano," he said, as if he'd read her mind. "We're in the same study hall."

"Oh, that's right. You're new this year." And a real babe, Deirdre thought to herself.

"Yeah. The new kid on the block." Jon brushed the hair off his forehead and glanced at the police cars. "I didn't know what to expect here. Not a murder, that's for sure. Did you know her?"

Deirdre nodded. "She's a cheerleader. A friend of my sister's. I mean, she *was* . . ." Deirdre stopped suddenly as a lump rose in her throat.

"Hey, I'm sorry," Jon said quickly. "I guess you were good friends with her too, huh?"

Deirdre swallowed hard. "No, but I still feel awful. And it's so scary. Just the idea that somebody sneaked into the gym and . . . and *murdered* her!"

"Yeah. Look, I can tell you're upset," he said softly. "I shouldn't have said anything about it."

"It's okay," Deirdre assured him. "How could you not say anything? It's all anybody's talking about."

"Right." He brushed his hair back again. His

thick brows drew together in a frown as his pale eyes swept over the parking lot.

"You probably wish you never transferred here," Deirdre said.

"No, not really," he replied. "Anything will be better than where I was before."

"Why? Where was that?"

Jon shrugged and glanced away. "You don't want to know. Let's just say I had some problems over there."

Deirdre studied him. Even though he wasn't big, he had broad shoulders and was built like an athlete. "I hope Shadyside turns out better," she told him.

"Yeah, so do I." He turned back to her, and a smile slowly spread across his face. "Thanks, Deirdre. Thanks for saying that." He seemed genuinely grateful. "Maybe sometime you and I . . ."

"Yeah. Maybe," she replied, feeling her heart start to pound.

Jon suddenly bent forward and peered closely at her face.

Deirdre felt her cheeks redden. "What are you staring at?"

"Well, since you have a twin, I don't want to get confused," he explained. He reached out and touched the mole on her cheek. "Does your sister have one of these, too?"

Deirdre shook her head. His finger felt cool

against her hot, blushing skin.

"You're the lucky one, then. It looks great." Jon dropped his hand and straightened up. "Listen, I have to go. I'll see you tomorrow."

Deirdre stared at him. Weird, she thought. What a weird thing to do. And then another thought flashed into her mind: It's the first time anyone ever told me I'm luckier than Dana.

She watched him walk away. She could still feel the cool touch of his finger on her chin.

She had a strong urge to follow him, to keep their conversation going.

But there will be time for that, she decided.

Maybe this morning's horror will be the end of it. Maybe things will be looking up from now on.

Chapter Four

The Vampire's First Drink

L ater, Deirdre sat with Stacy Malcolm and Jennifer Fear in The Corner, a hangout near Shadyside High. As they shared a double order of fries, they talked about the murder and about Trisha's frightening vision for the senior class. Then Deirdre told them about Gary's car accident.

"Trisha was with Gary again?" Stacy demanded. "How could Trisha do that to Mary?" Stacy and Mary O'Connor had become close friends since they were both on the track team.

"Why pick on Trisha? It's Gary's fault, too, you know," Jennifer told her.

"Maybe so, but Trisha shouldn't have anything to do with him," Stacy declared. "Not unless he totally breaks up with Mary."

"Will you forget about that for now?" Deirdre told her. "We were talking about Trisha's vision, remember? The Doomed Class? All of us dying off one by one?"

Stacy shot her a skeptical glance. "Come on, Deirdre. Gary's brakes were shot. So he plowed into that car. It wasn't some horrible prediction coming true. If it was, he and Trisha would both be dead."

"Isn't one murder enough for today?" Deirdre shrieked.

Stacy grabbed her hand. "Calm down," she whispered. "We're going to be okay, Deirdre. A whole class can't be doomed."

"That's what Dana said," Deirdre admitted, her heart pounding. "But I could tell she was freaked."

"Well, no wonder," Jennifer declared. "I mean, Dana found Danielle lying there in the gym. She must totally be in shock." She swept her long brown hair away from her face and shuddered. "Oh, stop. Please. Let's not talk about this any- more, okay?"

Deirdre nodded okay. Jennifer hated discussing stuff like fate and strange, mysterious deaths. She guessed it was because her last name was Fear.

Ever since Jennifer's ancestors had settled in Shadyside more than a hundred years before, there had been frightening stories about them.

They used dark magic to cast evil spells. . . .

They caused accidents and fires and deaths. . . . The whole family was evil. . . .

Deirdre shook her head. I've known Jennifer since kindergarten, she thought. She's just a regular person. But she can never be comfortable. She can never feel normal—because her name is Fear.

Deirdre finished her Coke and glanced around the small restaurant. Their waiter seemed to have disappeared.

Deirdre left the booth and went to the counter to order another Coke. As she waited, the door swung open and a girl with dark red hair and a heart-shaped face entered.

Jon Milano came in behind her.

Deirdre felt a stab of disappointment. I guess he wasn't as interested in me as I thought.

The redheaded girl swept past the counter and gazed around the crowded diner. She shrugged, then crossed to the CD jukebox and peered down at the selections.

As Deirdre turned away, Jon slipped up beside her and propped his elbows on the counter. "Hi. I didn't expect to see you again so soon."

"Hey, Jon." Deirdre felt his arm pressing against her shoulder. Her heart pumped a little harder. What is wrong with me? she asked herself. He obviously has a girlfriend already.

"I guess this place is a Shadyside hangout, huh?" he asked.

Deirdre nodded. "It gets really packed after

school." The waitress brought her Coke and she paid for it.

"Let me have one of those. To go," Jon told the girl.

One Coke? Was he with the redhead or not?

Jon shifted his weight. His arm pressed harder against her. Deirdre could feel it trembling. She glanced up and caught him staring at her. "What is it?" she asked.

"I wish I . . ." He took a long, slow breath. "Are you going with anyone?" he asked.

Deirdre glanced quickly toward the jukebox.

The redhead was gone.

He's not with her! Deirdre realized. It just looked that way.

Do I want to go out with him? Deirdre wondered. He's not Mickey. But Mickey hardly knows I'm alive. Besides, Dana is going with Mickey.

Dana and Mickey. Dana and Mickey . . .

So why do I find myself thinking about Mickey when I'm standing here talking to Jon?

"Uh . . . no. I'm not going with anyone," she told Jon.

His eyes brightened. "Great. I mean, well . . . see you later." He grabbed his Coke and a straw and hurried out the door.

Deirdre picked up her own Coke and started back to the table.

To her surprise, Mickey stood there, talking to Stacy and Jennifer.

She blinked. Was he a hallucination?

She thought about him—and there he was!

As Deirdre drew closer to the table, she saw the upset expressions on the girls' faces. Mickey turned to her, his face pale and frightened.

"Did you hear?" he choked out.

Deirdre gasped. "Is it Dana? Did something happen to my sister?"

Chapter Five

Words of the Vampire

"**N**o. Dana is okay," Mickey replied. "It's about Danielle. Did you hear what the police said on the radio news? About Danielle?"

"No. What?" Deirdre asked.

Mickey swallowed hard. Behind him, Stacy let out a sob. Jennifer leaned forward to comfort her.

"All of Danielle's blood had been drained," Mickey finally choked out. "Every last drop."

Deirdre's mouth opened in a horrified gasp. She stared at him, stunned.

"But—th-that's impossible," she stammered. "Dana said she didn't see any blood in the gym. Not anywhere. What happened to it? How could it all just disappear?"

Mickey shook his head. "Don't ask me. All I

know is, that's what I heard on the radio. It's so . . . weird. There wasn't a single drop of blood left in her body."

Deirdre sank into the booth beside Jennifer. Mickey slid across from her, next to Stacy.

"It might not be true," Jennifer murmured. "Maybe the news reporter got it wrong."

"You think?" Stacy asked quickly.

"But remember what Dana said?" Mickey replied softly. "She said Danielle was pale—*unbelievably* pale. Now we know why."

Deirdre felt sick. What *could* have happened to Danielle's blood?

There had to be a logical explanation. There *had* to be.

She closed her eyes, but it made the room spin. She opened them again.

As she gazed around the restaurant, her scalp suddenly prickled in fear. Dressed in black, Clark Dickson slipped like a shadow into a back booth, next to Debra Lake.

Count Clarkula, Deirdre thought with a shiver.

The name is supposed to be a joke.

The whole vampire act was supposed to be . . . a *joke*.

But look at those circles under Debra's eyes. She's changed so much since she started going out with Clark. She's still pretty, but she used to sparkle.

Now she looks dull. So tired and pale.

Deirdre shivered again. Dana told me that Clark appeared in the gym, two seconds after she found Danielle's body.

Was he there the whole time?

The blood was all drained from Danielle's body.

Drained . . .

Deirdre glanced at Clark's and Debra's booth again.

Count Clarkula . . .

Could Clark actually be a vampire?

No, that's crazy, she quickly told herself. There aren't any vampires.

That's *crazy*!

But what if he *thinks* he is? Deirdre wondered. What if he *wants* to be a vampire?

Maybe Clark really got into the vampire act. Too far into it.

Maybe it's not an act anymore.

Deirdre watched Debra murmur something to Clark. Then Debra slid out of their booth and went into the bathroom. Clark pulled a notebook from his backpack and began writing in it.

I'll go talk to Debra, Deirdre decided. Ask her what the deal is with Clark. Maybe she'll tell me she looks so pale and tired because she has the flu or something. That Clark is just shy and quiet and private. That I'm totally nuts.

Deirdre took a deep breath and began to slide out of the booth. She stood up too soon and bumped the table with her hip. As her half-filled glass of Coke teetered, she reached for it—and knocked it over with the back of her hand.

"Whoa!" Mickey shot out of his seat as a river of soda poured across the table.

"I'm sorry!" Deirdre cried.

She grabbed the rolling glass and set it upright, then tossed a paper napkin onto the puddle. "I'm such a klutz—I'm sorry!"

"Hey, relax," Mickey told her. "It's only Coke."

Flustered, Deirdre snatched up some more napkins and kept mopping up the mess. She felt too embarrassed to look at Mickey.

Dana would make a joke out of this, she thought. Why can't I?

Deirdre shoved the sopping napkins into the empty glass. "I have to do something," she murmured, not meeting Mickey's eyes. "I'll be back in a minute."

Deirdre turned from the table and hurried toward the bathroom.

Clark's booth was empty now.

The spiral notebook lay open on the table.

Deirdre glanced around and spotted Clark at the front counter. Debra stood beside him. She must have come out while I was cleaning up the Coke, Deirdre realized.

She edged closer to the booth and peered down at the notebook. And read the words scrawled in black ink across the paper.

The terrifying words:

"So cold. So pale,
You lie before me.
Your blood has vanished,
People say.
How? Where? they ask.
They don't ask me, but I could say.
Your blood gives life. . . ."

PART TWO

Chapter Six

Deirdre in Danger

"It has been three days since the body of high school senior Danielle Cortez was discovered in the Shadyside High gym," the TV newscaster declared.

Deirdre sat in a chair in Jennifer Fear's bedroom, gazing at the TV. On the screen they showed a picture of Danielle in her cheerleader uniform. Smiling and pretty.

Alive.

The school had held a memorial service for Danielle two days before. It was so awful, Deirdre thought. Everyone sat there feeling so sad . . . so terribly shocked and sad. But we all felt something else . . .

Fear.

"No blood was found at the scene," the

reporter continued. "And according to the coroner's report, no blood was left in the girl's body. So far the police have no suspects in what has been dubbed 'The Vampire Murder.'"

With a cry, Deirdre grabbed the remote and zapped the TV off. "I hate this!"

"I know. It's so awful." Jennifer leaned back against her headboard and frowned. "Did you tell anybody about Clark's poem?"

"Just you and Stacy. And Dana," Deirdre added. "Now Dana really thinks Clark might be the killer."

"Does she think he's a vampire, too?"

"I'm not sure. Maybe," Deirdre replied.

"Come on, Deirdre, there aren't any vampires," Jennifer insisted.

"I know that. But I told you—maybe Clark *thinks* he's one. That poem was so creepy!" Deirdre shuddered as she remembered the lines.

"Yeah. He's definitely weird," Jennifer agreed. "But the police questioned Clark for hours. And they don't consider him a suspect. I think it was some stranger. A real psycho with a thing about blood."

Deirdre shuddered again. "Danielle's funeral is tomorrow."

Jennifer sat up straight and ran her fingers through her long brown hair. "This is too depressing. Let's talk about something else."

"Like what?"

"Like Jon Milano," Jennifer suggested with a sly smile. "Did he ask you out yet?"

Deirdre shook her head. "I'm not even sure he's going to, either. I mean, I've seen him a dozen times in study hall. What's he waiting for?"

"Maybe he's shy."

"No way," Deirdre told her. "You should hear him talk about himself. Bragging about how he works out all the time and what great abs he has. Talking about how he's going to ace all his classes because Shadyside is so pitiful compared to his other school."

"So? He's a little conceited," Jennifer replied. She smiled. "I like conceited guys. Guys who are confident."

Deirdre sighed. "I can't figure him out."

"But you still have a thing for him?" Jennifer asked.

"Yeah, I guess." I can't help it, Deirdre thought. There's something about him . . .

Deirdre slid onto the floor and leaned against the chair. "Anyway, I still have a thing for Mickey, too," she confessed. "Not that *he's* interested. Every time he sees me now, he makes a crack about being drowned in Coke."

Jennifer studied her. "Does Dana know you like Mickey?"

"No way!" Dana said. "I don't talk about stuff like that with Miss Perfect. That would start world war three."

"Whoa." Jennifer's eyes widened. "You really can't talk to your sister?"

Deirdre bit her lip. "It's hard. I . . . I guess I'm a little jealous of Dana. We look alike, but she got the good personality."

"Oh, puh-lease!" Jennifer rolled her eyes. "You're quieter, that's all. And so what if Jon hasn't asked you out yet? Why don't you ask him?"

Deirdre sighed. I should, she thought. That's what Dana would do. . . .

Jennifer scooted off the bed and crossed the room to a shelf of CDs. As she picked through them, the door burst open and Stacy entered the room.

"Hi, where's Josie?" Deirdre asked. "I thought she was coming with you."

"Somebody called in sick at Pete's Pizza, so she had to fill in," Stacy replied. She pulled a bright orange beret off her head and sailed it onto the bed like a Frisbee. "Guess what? I just saw the girls' basketball schedule, and we play Waynesbridge first."

Jennifer groaned. "They *always* beat us!"

"Don't say that," Stacy protested. She flopped onto the bed. "It's bad luck."

"But it's true," Jennifer declared, opening one of the CDs. "We need some new talent. Someone eight feet tall!"

"There's a new girl in my English class—Anita

something," Stacy said. "Have you seen her? She's got red hair and she's really tall. Maybe we can talk her into trying out." Stacy propped herself up on her elbows and turned to Deirdre. "What about you?"

"That's right!" Jennifer agreed. "You were really good your sophomore year, Deirdre."

"Thanks, but my grades were the pits," Deirdre reminded her. "That's why I dropped off the team."

"But your grades are okay now, right?" Stacy asked. "You should try out. We really need you."

"Yeah, but what if I make the team and then my grades start to slide?" Deirdre argued. "I have to keep them up to get into college, you know."

Stacy rolled onto her back and gazed at the ceiling. "At least you can afford to go to any college you want," she said. "If I don't get a basketball scholarship, I'll get stuck going to a State school."

"You'll get a scholarship," Jennifer assured her. "You made all-state last year. You'll do it again this year."

"Thanks. It would be great to go to the tournament. Since this is our last year."

Jennifer sighed. "I wish we could start the year all over again. Everybody is so scared and upset. Do you think we'll still have the senior overnight this weekend?"

"I haven't heard anything," Deirdre replied,

shaking her head. "I hope it isn't canceled."

The senior camp-out in Fear Street Woods wasn't a school activity, but it *was* a tradition. Shadyside seniors had been doing it forever.

It won't feel right if we don't have the camp-out, she thought.

But then again, nothing about this year feels right so far.

As Deirdre drove home a little while later, she flipped on the radio. A reporter talked excitedly about Danielle's murder.

Deirdre changed the station. Same story.

Five o'clock, Deirdre thought. News time. And Danielle's death is the biggest story.

She snapped the radio off and drove the rest of the way home in silence.

Will we ever find out what happened? she wondered, as she let herself into her house. Will we ever know who killed her?

The phone rang as Deirdre climbed the stairs to her bedroom. She ran the rest of the way up and caught it on the third ring. "Hello?"

A voice said something she couldn't hear.

"Hello?" she repeated. "Could you talk a little louder?"

"Do you know who this is?" someone asked.

The voice was low, almost weak, as if the speaker had no strength. Cell phone, Deirdre thought, sitting down on the bed. "I think your batteries are low," she replied.

A soft, breathy laugh came over the line. "Do you know who I am?"

Deirdre shivered. The raspy whisper of a voice gave her the creeps. "No. Who?"

"Don't you want to guess? I'll give you a hint— Danielle's blood was delicious. And you're next."

Chapter Three

A Surprise in the Coffin

It's too nice a day for a funeral," Deirdre murmured, shaking her head.

Dana, walking a step behind her sister, raised a hand to her forehead to shield her eyes from the bright sunlight. She didn't reply to Deirdre.

Instead, she pictured Danielle. Danielle sprawled on her back on the gym floor . . . her long, black hair spread under her head like a blanket.

Her eyes staring blankly. Like glass. Like cold, empty glass.

And her face . . . so pale . . . ghostly . . . drained.

Deirdre's voice floated into Dana's thoughts. "How can Danielle be dead? She was so full of life. She had more energy than the rest of the cheerleader squad put together."

Dana sighed. "Tell me about it," she replied, rolling her eyes. "We'd be totally wrecked after practicing for hours. And Danielle would be there, saying, 'Come on, girls. Let's rehearse it one more time.' She was . . . incredible," Dana said, the words catching in her throat.

"We're just teenagers," Deirdre said, adjusting the sleeves of her white, pleated blouse. "How can someone we know be *dead*? People our age don't die—do they?"

A bitter laugh escaped Dana's throat. "Yes . . . if they're *murdered*."

Murder.

A chill rolled down Dana's back. Was it the word? *Murder*? Or was it the anger she felt?

The furious anger that someone had invaded their high school. Someone sick and twisted. Someone *evil*.

This *creature* came into their school and took the life of someone they knew and cared about.

One of us, Dana thought, unable to keep a hot tear from sliding down her burning cheek. One of us . . .

One of us . . .

Deirdre took Dana's hand as they crossed the street. The big stone church loomed between two rows of tall poplars. The shadow of the cross on its steeple fell over the shimmering green grass.

Dana thought of Trisha.

She remembered Trisha's gloomy prediction. "I had a vision," Trisha told them. She had visions and psychic flashes all the time.

But never one as frightening as this.

"We're all going to die, one by one. The senior class is cursed."

Dana didn't take her seriously. Most kids didn't.

Trisha was well-liked, in spite of her odd flashes and predictions. She was such a good person. So warm and caring.

No one would ever guess from her attitude that her father was a billionaire. That her family had to be the richest in Shadyside.

Trisha never acted stuck-up or special.

She could have gone to any of the fanciest private schools in the country. But Trisha chose to stay with her friends at Shadyside High.

So even if Dana never believed Trisha's constant stream of strange dreams and psychic flashes, she didn't hold them against her. She didn't put her down for them or call her crazy or weird.

Trisha was Trisha.

Stepping into the shadow of the cross on the church lawn, Dana blinked. And saw Trisha standing there. She had a silky, blue top pulled down over a straight black skirt. Her blond hair was pulled back tightly behind her head.

Her eyes were red-rimmed, her normally smooth cheeks puffy. Trisha's hands were clasped tightly together over a wadded-up tissue.

She moved to hug Dana. Then wrapped Deirdre in the same hug. "I don't want to go in there," she sobbed, motioning toward the church.

Two men in dark suits stood at either side of the entrance. One of them helped a white-haired woman up the single step.

Josie Maxwell came up the walk with Jennifer Fear. Both girls had dark hats pulled down over their hair. Both had their eyes hidden behind sunglasses.

Deirdre hugged them both.

Dana hung back. Her heart was heaving against her chest. She knew if she didn't hold on tight to her emotions, she'd totally lose it. Explode in wailing sobs and a flood of bitter tears.

Keep it together, she ordered herself.

Danielle is dead. My tears won't bring her back.

"I was inside," Trisha told them. "But I had to come out."

"It's so awful!" Josie declared. "I feel as if I'm in a bad dream."

Jennifer lowered her head. She was a quiet girl. She seldom spoke when a lot of people were around. She bit her lip. Her eyes gazed at the shadowy grass.

"Danielle's mother is in there, sobbing her eyes out," Trisha reported. "She's all alone now.

Danielle's brother is somewhere in the Middle East. He's in the Air Force. And Danielle's father died last year."

"Oh, wow," Josie murmured. "Wow."

"We've got to go inside," Deirdre said. "We can't stand out here all afternoon."

"First day of school," Josie muttered. "How could it happen on the first day of school?"

"How could it happen at all?" Dana murmured.

She felt a powerful weight in her chest. All that emotion. . . all that sadness and anger, trying to burst out.

She squeezed Deirdre's arm, and held onto her sister, as if holding onto life. Something real. Something warm.

The girls clung together, hugging themselves, standing in the shadow of the tall cross, glancing at the open church doors, the two men standing so somberly at the entrance, like guards at the gates of death.

A plane roared high overhead. The sound jarred Dana from her unhappy thoughts. She blinked and shook her head, as if waking up.

"Come on, everyone," she urged softly. "Take a deep breath. Let's go inside and get this over with."

The sweet-sour smell of lilies greeted them as they stepped into the church. Dana gasped.

The aroma was so heavy. She felt as if she were suffocating.

Suffocating . . .

She pictured poor Danielle. Not breathing . . . not breathing . . .

Dana followed the others into the chapel. Her eyes swept over the stained glass windows. . . the statuary in front of the altar. . . the coffin.

Danielle's coffin.

It appeared to float like a dark canoe on a sea of white and yellow lilies.

The coffin lid stood open. Dana could see the red satin covering on the inside of the lid.

She glanced away. She didn't want to see Danielle lying in there. Danielle's pretty face. Danielle's smile. . .

No. No more smiles.

Did they have to leave the coffin open?

Dana followed her sister into a pew near the back. Josie led the way, followed by Jennifer, then Deirdre, then Dana. They slid along the smooth wooden bench until there was room for everyone to sit.

Dana's eyes swept over the pews. She saw Stacy Malcolm and Mary O'Connor sitting a few rows ahead. Then she saw several Shadyside teachers clustered together on the other side of the chapel. In front of them, she recognized several parents of kids in their class.

She turned and saw Mickey enter the chapel, wearing dark slacks and a dark sports jacket over an open white shirt. Josh Maxwell, Josie's stepbrother, walked beside him. Matty Winger trailed a few steps behind them, scratching his curly, dark hair, looking very uncomfortable.

Dana waved to Mickey. But he was talking to Josh and didn't see her. She turned back to the front, clasping and unclasping her clammy, cold hands in her lap. She tried desparately to keep her eyes off the casket.

I hate the smell of lilies, Dana thought. I'll never forget this smell, so sweet and heavy and unpleasant. I know I'll remember it for the rest of my life.

Organ music played softly from behind the altar. Rising up over the music were loud sobs from the front pew. Dana squinted to the front— and saw Mrs. Cortez, Danielle's mother, head lowered, buried in her hands, her shoulders heaving up and down as she cried.

When the music ended, the sobs continued.

The funeral began. A middle-aged minister with a mane of white hair stepped forward carrying a Bible and began to speak.

Dana didn't hear much of what he had to say. The funeral passed quickly for her in a soft blur of flowers and saddened faces, the heavy aroma of the lilies, the steady, painful sobs of Danielle's mother.

And the sight of the open coffin.

A face inside. A girl.

A girl Dana knew.

The lid standing up so straight. Open. Open. As if Danielle were expected to climb out and join the rest of them in the pews.

Crazy thoughts, Dana scolded herself.

Before she realized it, the service had ended. Two hymns were sung. The somber organ chords continued as people rose to their feet.

Everyone moved down the aisle, to the altar.

Dana swallowed hard. She tried to think clearly. She tried to focus.

What is happening now? Why is everyone going to the front?

She hadn't been to many funerals. It took her a while to realize that people were filing past the open coffin, saying goodbye to Danielle.

Oh no. I can't! she thought.

And then she knew she had to.

She pressed close to Deirdre, who kept wiping her eyes with a shredded tissue. And waited as the line moved slowly, so slowly. Organ chords and tearful sobs surrounding them.

Closer to the coffin. The red satin glowing inside the lid.

"It will all be over in a few seconds," Deirdre whispered in Dana's ear. "Then we can go home."

Dana nodded.

Two young men leaned over the coffin. Dana had never seen them before. One of them ran his hand along the coffin edge. The other dropped a single, long-stemmed rose into the coffin.

Then they moved on. And it was Dana and Deirdre's turn.

Dana took a deep breath and held it. She gathered up all her courage and turned to gaze at Danielle's body.

Danielle wore a long, purple dress with a frilly blouse. Her long, black hair was tied neatly behind her head. Her eyes were shut. Her arms rested stiffly at her sides.

"It doesn't look like Danielle at all," Deirdre whispered. "Why is she so orange?"

Yes, Dana saw, Danielle's skin was bright orange. Not natural. Not right.

Not Danielle.

Her lips were painted bright red and set in a strange smile. And her face . . . her face glowed like the skin of an orange.

Dana couldn't help herself. She stopped at the coffin-side and stared. Why couldn't they at least make her *pink*? Why was she this awful, ugly color?

"Ohhhh." A low moan escaped Dana's throat. And her mouth dropped open—as she saw the orange begin to fade on Danielle's face.

The color faded . . . washed away.

Fainter . . . fainter . . . until all traces of the orange were gone. And Danielle's skin was a dull blue. A cold, cold blue.

And then as Dana gaped in shocked horror, Danielle's eyes popped open.

Danielle raised her head off the red satin with a groan. Her glassy dark eyes fixed on Dana.

And her bright red lips parted.

Opened.

And a plea—a whisper like the wind—came from somewhere far away, somewhere deep inside Danielle.

"*Help me,*" the dead girl whispered to Dana.

"*Help me. I can't sleep.*"

Chapter Eight

The Vampire Revealed

"T his . . . isn't . . . happening," Dana murmured out loud.

She stared, frozen in terror. Stared at the blue-skinned face, the glassy black eyes gazing so blankly up at her.

Danielle's blood-red lips. Quivering. Opening just wide enough to get the choked, dry words out:

"*I can't sleep. Help me.*"

No.

No way.

With a gasp, Dana turned away from the coffin. Turned sharply to her sister. "I'm imagining that—"

No. Not imagining.

Deirdre grasped Dana's arm. Squeezed it so tightly.

Deirdre, with her face twisted in horror, gaping

wide-eyed into the coffin, into the corpse's pleading face.

Deirdre saw it, too.

It wasn't a hallucination. Not Dana's horrifying nightmare.

Deirdre saw it too.

Dana spun away. Ran up the aisle. She only wanted to escape this unspeakable horror. She only wanted to forget.

But Deirdre stayed. Deirdre watched the corpse settle back on its red satin pillow. Deirdre watched Danielle's eyes close and the color, the bright, orange color, return to her cheeks.

Deirdre stayed. And determined right then and there to help the poor dead girl.

"Don't worry, Danielle," she whispered. "I heard you. I'll do what I can."

"We have to have a seance tonight at Jennifer's house," Deirdre explained to her friends when they arrived at her house after the funeral.

Jennifer wanted no part of it.

But Deirdre told her they had no choice. "Dana and I both saw her sit up," she explained.

Josie gasped. Trisha shut her eyes and covered her mouth with her hand.

"She begged us to help her," Deirdre told them. "She said she couldn't sleep."

Dana ran away and locked herself in her bedroom.

That left Deirdre, Jennifer, Trisha, and Josie.

"We have to try to reach Danielle," Deirdre insisted breathlessly. "Maybe she can't sleep because she wants to reveal the murderer to us."

"But why do we have to do it at my house?" Jennifer demanded. "Just because I'm a Fear, doesn't mean that I have special powers. I can't contact the dead."

"I know," Deirdre replied. "But that library in your house . . . that creepy little room . . . all those old books. It is the only place I know where we have a chance of reaching Danielle in the spirit world."

Jennifer shook her head. "I'll let you do it," she replied. "I'll even join in. But you know I don't believe in this stuff." She turned to Josie, who had been silent all along. "How about you, Josie?"

Deirdre saw Josie swallow hard. Josie suddenly looked so pale, pale as a corpse.

"I . . . I don't know," Josie stammered, not looking any of them in the eye. "I never planned to go back to that room in your house, Jennifer. I had a bad experience there. When we were goofing around with different curses. I think I might have done something there . . ." Her voice trailed off.

"What? What are you talking about?" Jennifer demanded impatiently.

Josie shook her head. "Never mind." She raised her eyes to Deirdre. "When do you want to meet?"

"Let's go now," Trisha said eagerly. She glanced across the street at the church. The doors had been closed. Everyone else had either gone on to the burial at the cemetery or had gone home.

"No. Tonight," Deirdre insisted. "We'll meet at Jennifer's tonight. We'll follow the seance instructions in that book we found last time we were there."

"And we'll talk to Danielle," Trisha said with enthusiasm. "We can do it. I know we can."

The others stared at her thoughtfully, each girl swimming in her own troubled sea of thoughts. No one said a word as they turned to go home.

Deirdre was surprised when Josie called her a few minutes later.

Deirdre had been arguing with Dana, trying to persuade Dana to come to the seance. "You and I were the only ones who saw her," Deirdre insisted. "The only ones who know that her spirit cannot rest. We owe it to Danielle."

"You're crazy, Deirdre!" Dana shot back. "The whole idea is crazy."

She startled Deirdre by grabbing both of her shoulders. "I want to have a normal senior year—do you hear me?" she cried heatedly. "I want a normal life. No seances. No talking to the dead. I want to forget what happened today. I *have* to forget it. Or else I'll go crazy!"

Dana shrieked the last words.

Deirdre pulled free. "Okay, okay," she said softly, rubbing her shoulders. She could still feel her sister's fingers digging into her skin. "I understand. I really do. But aren't you curious? Don't you want to see—?"

And then Deirdre's phone rang. She hurried into her room to answer it. She heard Dana's door slam down the hall.

"Josie? What's wrong?" Deirdre asked breathlessly.

"About the seance," Josie started. "I didn't want to say it in front of the others. But I'm frightened to go back to that house."

"Excuse me?" Deirdre carried the phone over to the bed and plopped down hard on the bedspread. "You're afraid to go to Jennifer's? You mean, because she's a Fear?"

"No. Of course not," Josie replied. "You don't remember. Last June. Just before Trisha's big party . . ."

"What about it?" Deirdre demanded impatiently. What was Josie trying to tell her? Why was she acting so odd?

A long silence.

"I don't really want to talk about it," Josie said finally. "But . . . remember we were in the library, fooling around with curses and old spells?"

Deirdre lay back, let her head sink into the pillow. "Yeah. I remember that afternoon."

"Well, I finished the Doom Spell," Josie said in a trembling voice. "I . . . I don't know what I did. I called up something evil . . . and . . . and . . ."

"Take it easy, Josie," Deirdre said softly. She sat up. "You sound really messed up. Do you want me to come over?"

"No. That's okay," Josie replied. "I mean . . . well . . . Don't you see, Deirdre? Everything . . . Everything that's happened . . . It *might be all my fault!*"

"Huh? That's impossible," Deirdre replied, trying to sound soothing.

Doom Spell? *Her* fault?

What was Josie talking about?

"If we reach Danielle tonight, she'll straighten everything out," Deirdre told her. "She'll tell us who murdered her. She'll tell us who the vampire is. You—you've got to come tonight, Josie. You've got to—okay?"

"Okay. I guess."

She sounded very frightened.

And that night they sat cross-legged on the floor, closed up in the library in Jennifer Fear's house, the room crammed from floor to ceiling with old books of magic and the occult.

Deirdre, Jennifer, Trisha, and Josie.

The light from a dozen black candles flickering all around them. Shadows dancing over their somber, intent faces.

They held hands. And shut their eyes.

And invoked the spirits, calling to those just beyond the living. Calling to the restless souls who could not sleep.

Calling to Danielle.

"Talk to us, Danielle," Deirdre whispered.

"*Talk to us. Talk to us,*" the other three chanted.

"We have come to help you, Danielle," Deirdre said.

"*Talk to us. Talk to us.*"

"We know you cannot sleep. Tell us why, Danielle. We want to help you. Tell us why you cannot sleep."

"*Talk to us. Talk to us.*"

All four girls gasped as a high, shrill voice floated up from the darkness. Distant at first, soft as wind against tree leaves. And then stronger, strong enough to hear.

"*Yessssssssss.*"

Deirdre opened her eyes, expecting to see someone. A spirit. Shadow. Danielle.

But no. The dancing candle light revealed no one.

"Danielle—is that you?" Deirdre choked out, her heart thudding.

"*Yessssssss.*"

"Danielle, we're . . . here!" Deirdre cried. "We came to help you."

Silence for a long moment. And then:

"*I cannot see you. I am not with you yet. Who is there? Who is calling me?*"

Josie squeezed Deirdre's hand. "Is it Danielle?" she whispered to Deirdre. "Do you really think it's Danielle?"

"Of course it is," Trisha snapped. "Ssshh. Let her talk. This is amazing!"

"*Who is in the room?*" the eerie, distant voice demanded again.

The girls called out their names, going around the circle.

Silence again. Then the sound of a strong wind.

Deirdre felt a swirl of cold air around her. The air smelled sour, like decayed meat.

The smell of death?

"*I am a spirit that cannot rest,*" the voice announced finally.

"We want to help you, Danielle," Deirdre replied. She caught the frightened expression on Josie's face. Next to Josie, Trisha looked excited, thrilled—not frightened at all. Jennifer kept her face down. Deirdre couldn't read her expression at all.

"Let us help you," Deirdre urged the spirit.

"*How can you help someone from the other side?*" the voice demanded, soft again, from so far away.

"Tell us who murdered you," Trisha blurted out. "Danielle—tell us."

"Tell us who the vampire is," Deirdre added.

"Tell us so that you can rest."

"Yesssssss," the voice hissed.

"Who—who is it?" Trisha asked.

"Who is the vampire, Danielle? Who did this to you? Who murdered you?"

Silence.

A long, long silence.

Sitting straight up on the floor, her entire body tensed, every muscle tight, Deirdre felt another blast of cold, foul-smelling air.

And then, finally, the spirit's voice floated through the tiny room once again.

"Trisha is the murderer," the voice whispered. *"Trisha is the vampire!"*

Chapter Nine

A Joke?

"Nooooo!"

Trisha uttered a howl of protest. She leaped to her feet.

"Danielle—what are you *saying*?" she cried. "It isn't true! It *isn't*! Why are you saying that?"

The spirit replied with a shriek of laughter— ugly, cold laughter. Inhuman laughter.

"*Trisha is the vampire! Trisha is the murderer!*" And then, another long symphony of cruel, cackling laughter.

Trisha backed to the wall, trembling, hands clenched into tight fists.

"Why?" she demanded. "Danielle—why are you accusing me?"

Deirdre jumped to her feet. She wrapped Trisha in a hug. "Don't you see?" Deirdre asked softly. "Don't you see? It's not Danielle."

"Huh?" Trisha's mouth dropped open. Her whole body shook.

"It's not Danielle!" Deirdre screamed.

More high, shrill laughter rang out, echoing off the old bookshelves.

Josie and Jennifer were on their feet now. In the flickering candlelight, Deirdre could see the terror on their faces.

"You're not Danielle!" Deirdre called out to the cackling spirit. "You're playing a cruel joke. You're not our friend!"

"*Trisha did it! Trisha did it! Hahahahaha! Who is Trisha anyway?*"

"Turn on the light!" Deirdre screamed. "Get away, spirit. Get out of here!" She turned back to Trisha. "Only a joke. Don't you see? Only a horrible joke."

Jennifer clicked on the ceiling light. And pushed open the door to the hallway.

All four girls blinked in the bright light.

"Are you gone?" Deirdre called to the spirit. "Are you gone now?"

No reply.

"It—it was so awful!" Trisha cried. "To be accused like that. I—I thought it was Danielle. I thought she really believed that I—"

Deirdre wrapped her in another hug. "It's okay. We're all okay. The spirit—whoever she was—she's gone."

"Such a mean joke . . ." Trisha murmured, still trembling.

"It's over," Deirdre repeated.

Jennifer and Josie were back down on the floor now, blowing out the candles. Jennifer picked up the black candleholders and returned them to their shelf.

"I—I have to get out of here," Josie gasped. "This . . . this was all . . . too much." She started to the door.

"This didn't happen," Trisha called after her.

Josie turned back. "Huh?"

"It didn't happen," Trisha repeated, crossing her arms over her chest. "We weren't here. We didn't do this. Let's just pretend it never happened—okay?"

"Okay," Josie agreed. "Fine with me."

"This whole episode—it's over," Trisha continued. "From now on, everything will be normal. We'll go to the senior camp-out, and we'll have a great time. And everything will be normal. Right?"

"Normal," all four girls repeated in unison.

Deirdre followed them out. She wanted to believe it. She wanted the rest of senior year to be normal.

Was it possible?

She wasn't so sure.

PART THREE

Chapter Ten

Horror at the Campfire

Dana sat cross-legged on the dirt and gazed at the campfire blazing in a big clearing in Fear Street Woods. Mickey sat behind her, his muscular arms draped over her shoulders.

Music blared from a boom box. The sweet aroma of burning wood and roasting hot dogs drifted through the clearing.

"This is *excellent*." Mickey leaned closer and kissed Dana's ear. "Isn't it?" he whispered.

"Mmm." Dana shivered with pleasure as he kissed her again. "I was afraid we wouldn't have the overnight at all, after . . . what happened. I'm so glad they didn't cancel it. We all needed a little fun."

As Mickey nuzzled her neck, Dana gazed around the clearing.

Her sister Deirdre sat on one of the big logs arranged around the fire, talking to a good-looking guy with thick, dark hair and a lean, serious face.

"That's the new guy," Dana said. "Jon. I think Deirdre likes him."

Dana watched Jon slip his arm around Deirdre's shoulders. "Ha. They look pretty cozy. I hope Deirdre goes with it. He's kind of cute."

"Hey. Don't go getting any ideas about other guys," Mickey protested.

Dana laughed. "He's not my type. Too serious-looking."

Dana gave Mickey a quick kiss, then turned back to the clearing. Kenny Klein and Jade Feldman stood close to the fire, their arms around each other. Ty Sullivan and Mira Block sat with their backs against a big log, making out in a major way.

Stacy was talking to Mary O'Connor and Gary Fresno. Dana glanced at Trisha, who was busy roasting hot dogs with Josie and Jennifer.

Trisha kept her eye on Gary. And Gary kept glancing over Mary's shoulder at Trisha.

Is he going to break up with Mary? Dana wondered. He should dump her already! Mary knows all about Trisha.

Josh Maxwell sat on a big log, staring glumly at the flames. Marla Newman sat next to him, carrying on a one-sided conversation. Good luck,

Marla, Dana thought. I don't think Josh is over Debra yet.

"Debra isn't here, is she?" Dana asked. "Is she sick?"

"Who knows?" Mickey rested his chin on top of Dana's head. "Count Clarkula showed up, though."

"Huh?" Dana stared at Clark, who stood at the edge of the clearing, gazing into the dark woods. "Weird. He never comes to things like this."

"Yeah. Hey, who's that?" Mickey pointed to a girl who had burst out laughing. A tall, slender girl, with dark red hair and a heart-shaped face.

"She's new here, too," Dana told Mickey. "Her name is Anita Black. We're in calculus together."

Dana watched Anita laughing at Matty Winger. In typical nerdy fashion, Matty was pretending to swallow a flaming marshmallow.

"Matty is such a loser," Dana declared. "Did you know he called Deirdre on Thursday and pretended to be a vampire? He told her Danielle's blood was delicious and he was going to drink Deirdre's next. Yuck."

"Nice guy," Mickey snickered. "Same kind of call he made to Josh last summer, huh?"

Dana sneered. "You'd think maybe he could come up with something new!"

"Wait a sec. Did you say he called on Thursday?" Mickey asked.

"Yes," Dana replied. "Thursday afternoon. It was about five, I think."

"Then it couldn't have been Matty," Mickey told her. "I had a band rehearsal then, and we didn't quit until six. Matty was there the whole time."

Dana twisted around and stared at him. "Are you sure?"

"Positive."

"Then who made that disgusting call?" Dana wondered.

"Some sicko, I guess." Mickey tightened his arms around her. "Anyway, forget about it," he murmured into her ear.

Someone cranked up the boom box, and a bunch of kids began dancing in a big circle around the campfire.

"We're missing the dancing," Dana said.

"Who cares?" Mickey whispered. "This is more fun."

Dana shifted sideways and kissed him on the lips.

Kids were singing now as they danced, shouting the words at the top of their lungs.

Dana wrapped her arms around Mickey's neck and kissed him harder. He's right, she thought, closing her eyes. This is much more fun.

The pounding drumbeat echoed off the trees. The singing and shouting grew even louder.

Then a single sound rose over all the other noise.

A shrill cry of panic.

Dana opened her eyes and gasped as the figure of a girl scrambled out of the campfire.

A burning girl, with orange flames over her arms and legs and swirling around her head.

"Deirdre!" Dana shrieked. "She's on fire!"

Chapter Eleven

A Special Night

What is happening? What is happening?

At first Deirdre staggered in blind confusion, unwilling to believe the flames were real.

And then, as the shock wore off, she opened her mouth in screams of horror. "Help! Oh, please—help!"

She began batting frantically at the flames swirling over her. "Help me!"

I'm going to die! her mind shrieked. I'm going to burn to death!

She heard a sizzling sound, so close, so close to her ears. A bitter odor invaded her nose.

My hair! Ohhhhh, my hair.

Deirdre shot her hands up and slapped frantically at her head.

Flames swept up her sleeve, scorching the

cotton, turning it black.

A searing pain tore through the skin on her arm. Deirdre twisted and shrieked in agony.

"Oh—!" Someone shoved her hard from behind. She fell to her knees, then toppled forward onto her stomach.

Before she could move, something thick and heavy landed on top of her. She felt strong arms wrap around her and hold her close.

I can't breathe! she thought. She knew someone was there, trying to put the fire out. But she felt trapped and helpless.

Her arm throbbed with pain.

"Is she okay?" Deirdre heard Dana's trembling cry. Dana sounded so far away. "Did you get to her in time?"

"I think so," a guy's voice replied.

Who? Who?

Jon's voice?

The heavy cover was peeled back. A sleeping bag, Deirdre realized.

Deirdre stared up into Jon's worried face.

Everyone stood around him, staring at her anxiously.

She gulped in some fresh air and began to cry. Her whole body shook violently.

"Deirdre!" Dana dropped to her knees. She started to grab Deirdre's shoulder, then snatched her hand back. "Are you burned? Does it hurt?"

Deirdre struggled to sit up and gasped in pain.

"You *are* hurt! Where?" Dana asked frantically.

"My. . . my arm." Deirdre bit her lip as Jon helped her sit up. She clutched her arm and rocked back and forth.

"Let me see it," Jon said. He quickly took a handful of ice from one of the coolers and held it against her arm. Deirdre shivered.

"I don't think it's too bad," Jon said after a moment. "It's not blistered."

"My hair . . ." Deirdre moaned. "Is it. . . ?"

"Just a little singed," Dana replied. "You were so. . . lucky."

Jon pulled the sleeping bag around Deirdre's shoulders. She leaned against him.

"Let's get you home," Dana declared. "We'll call Dr. Franks."

"She's right," Trisha agreed.

"No way," Deirdre told them. She didn't want to move at all, not with Jon holding her like this. "You heard Jon—it's not a bad burn. I'm okay. Really. And I don't want to miss the rest of the camp-out."

Jon saved my life, Deirdre thought, gazing up at him. He acted so quickly. He's so smart. . . so caring.

"What happened anyway?" Jennifer asked. "How did you fall into the fire?"

"I. . . I'm not sure," Deirdre stammered. "I don't remember too clearly. I think maybe someone bumped into me."

"I'm so sorry!" a voice cried. "Really. I feel so

74

horrible. This is all my fault!"

Deirdre gazed up as a tall, red-haired girl stepped closer. As she moved nearer, Deirdre recognized Anita Black.

"I tripped when we were all dancing," Anita explained. "I can't believe I'm such a klutz. I tried to catch my balance, but I couldn't. I crashed into you and. . ." She broke off, her lips quivering. "I feel just awful."

She's the girl who came into the restaurant ahead of Jon, Deirdre realized.

Do they know each other? I don't think so.

"It was an accident," Deirdre told her. She leaned back against Jon's shoulder. "Don't blame yourself, Anita. I feel okay. Really."

Anita covered her face with both hands. Her shoulders trembled. "If there's anything I can do. . ." she murmured.

Jon and Dana helped Deirdre over to one of the fat logs surrounding the campfire.

Gradually the pain began to ease. Jon's fingers were cool and gentle as he put a loose gauze bandage over the burn.

Slowly, the crowd drifted away. Dana stuck around for another minute. Then she and Mickey circled the fire and sat down again.

Someone turned the music up, and a few kids began dancing.

Jon squeezed Deirdre's shoulder. "I'll be back in a sec."

Deirdre shrugged off the sleeping bag and glanced down at herself.

Black scorch marks darkened one leg of her jeans and the front of her sweatshirt.

She felt her hair. The ends were stiff and frizzy.

I'm a total mess, she thought. She closed her eyes and breathed deeply. A faint smell of chocolate drifted through the air. She opened her eyes.

Jon stood over her, holding a cardboard container of cocoa.

"Thanks." Deirdre took the cup and started to drink.

"It's hot—don't burn yourself," Jon told her. "Oops. Bad choice of words."

Deirdre laughed. "At least you warned me." She carefully sipped some of the hot chocolate. "This tastes great."

He sat down beside her. "How are you feeling?"

"Okay. My arm is still throbbing. But it's not too bad. Jon? Thanks," Deirdre told him. "You saved my life."

"I just got to you first." He scooted closer and put his arm around her shoulder. "I'm just glad I was there."

Deirdre glanced up at him. His pale eyes seemed to glow. His lips came close, and before she realized what was happening, he kissed her.

Deirdre kissed him back. She felt his arms go around her. Holding her tight. He kissed her harder. His lips moved softly across her cheek.

Deirdre expected the kiss to continue. But he suddenly pulled back.

Deirdre stared at him, confused. "What's wrong?"

"Nothing," he replied, avoiding her gaze.

Something is wrong, Deirdre thought. *He suddenly looks so nervous. Or maybe he just doesn't like making out in the middle of a big crowd. I guess I don't, either.*

But I definitely liked kissing him.

"You want to go for a walk or something?" she asked.

"Sure. Good idea." Jon stood up. "Come on, I'll show you something I found in the woods."

Taking her hand, Jon pulled her to her feet. Deirdre drained the cocoa and tossed the cup into the campfire.

Then, still feeling shaky and weak, her legs trembling, she followed Jon out of the clearing and into the darkness of Fear Street Woods.

Deirdre began to shiver as they walked single file along a narrow path. Weeds snagged at her jeans, and low-hanging branches caught in her hair. Drops of water falling from the trees felt cold on her forehead.

This isn't exactly what I had in mind, she thought. "How far is it, Jon?"

"Not much farther." Jon reached back and caught her hand, twisting his fingers through hers.

Deirdre kept walking with him, deep into the woods. "It's kind of creepy back here," she murmured. "Maybe we should go back."

Jon stopped walking and pulled her alongside him. "There it is," he declared.

Following his gaze, Deirdre saw a small, wooden cabin, faintly lit up by the moon. Weathered and sagging, it stood in what had once been another big clearing. But the woods were slowly creeping back. Bushes and weeds brushed up against the cabin walls, and vines twisted around the crumbling stone chimney.

"Cool, huh?" Jon asked. "Someone must have built it a long time ago and abandoned it."

"How did you find it?"

"I went exploring when I first moved here," he replied. "It looks like a wreck, but I fixed it up a little inside. The fireplace even works."

"Really? Let's go in." Deirdre started toward the cabin.

"No, wait." Jon grabbed her hand and pulled her back. "Listen. I think I hear somebody."

Deirdre heard leaves rustling and twigs snapping. Then a voice called out, "Deirdre? Deirdre!"

"It's my sister," Deirdre said. "She must have gotten worried. She knows I don't like the woods that much."

"Deirdre, where are you?" Dana called. "Deirdre, answer me!"

"Dana, I'm okay!" Deirdre shouted. "Jon and I went for a walk, that's all!"

"Oh!" Dana giggled. "Sorry!"

Jon squeezed Deirdre's hand. "Maybe we should go back."

"Yeah." The mood is wrecked anyway, Deirdre thought.

They started back, but Jon stopped suddenly and spun her around to face him. "Don't tell anybody about the cabin, okay?" he asked.

"Huh? Why not?"

Jon's eyes flashed. "Because it's my special place," he declared. "I like to come here and think. You know. Escape the human race for a while."

"Well, if it's that important, then sure," Deirdre replied. "I won't tell anyone."

"Good." Jon brushed his fingers across her lips. "It will be our secret." He kissed her again.

Deirdre felt her heart jump. What a night! she thought. I had no idea it would turn out to be so special.

Dana lay in the tent and listened to the soft breathing sounds coming from the other sleeping bags. Jade and Greta were obviously asleep.

Everybody is asleep, Dana thought drowsily. Outside, she heard leaves rustling in the breeze and the faint peep of a night bird.

She wondered what time it was. Probably three-thirty or four, at least. They hadn't crawled into the tents until after two.

She thought about tomorrow. A campfire

breakfast. Then a hike in the woods. Marla said everybody had to get up early for it. Marla always wants to be in charge, Dana thought. But the hike would be fun.

Did I bring that extra pair of jeans?

She couldn't remember. Maybe she should check her duffel bag. But she felt so warm, so sleepy. Too sleepy to get up.

Her eyelids drooped shut.

The night bird chirped again.

As Dana rolled onto her back, she sensed something.

A presence. Not Greta or Jade. Someone else.

Mickey? she thought with a sly smile. Is he sneaking into our tent?

Dana felt something press against her bare throat.

Then a sting on the side of her neck.

A sharp, painful sting.

She flinched and tried to scream.

No sound came out. She couldn't even open her mouth.

It's a dream, she told herself as her heart pounded in panic. Just a dream.

Dana struggled to open her eyes. To sit up and shake off the dream. But her eyelids wouldn't lift.

She tried to sit up again, but her arms and legs felt heavy as lead.

I'm too weak to move! she thought. Why can't I wake up? What is happening to me?

Chapter Twelve

The Night Visitor

"**N**ooo!" Dana fumbled with her sleeping bag, trying to throw it off. It felt so heavy. She could hardly lift it. "Help me! Help!"

A hand grabbed her shoulder.

"Dana, what's wrong?" Jade cried out.

"What happened?" Greta demanded, scrambling over to her. "Are you hurt or something?"

A flashlight came on, shining in Dana's face. Still gasping in fear, she cupped a hand over her eyes and peered around.

Jade lowered her flashlight and peered back anxiously. She and Greta gazed at Dana, faces tight with worry.

"What happened?" Jade asked. "You scared us to death. Are you okay?"

Before Dana could reply, someone pulled back the tent flap.

"Clark!" Deirdre gasped as Clark Dickson's lean face appeared in the opening. "What are you doing here?"

"I—I couldn't sleep," he stammered. "I took a walk."

"In the Fear Street Woods? By yourself?" Greta asked.

"Why not? What could happen?" Clark's dark eyes locked intently on Dana. "I was passing by your tent and heard a scream. I think everybody did. Listen."

Dana suddenly became aware of other voices outside. Murmurs and conversations in the other tents. I woke the whole senior class, she thought with a sigh.

"Tell everybody I had a nightmare, would you?" she asked Clark. At least that will get rid of him, she thought.

His intense stare made her uncomfortable. And she remembered Deirdre's story, about the notebook in the restaurant . . . about Clark's weird, frightening poem.

Clark kept watching her. "Is that what it was— a nightmare?"

"What else could it have been?" Dana snapped. "Now, could you tell them before they all pile in here, please?"

"Sure." Clark backed out of the opening, letting the tent flap drop behind him.

"It must have been a horrible nightmare," Greta

declared as she and the others began to settle back into their sleeping bags. "What was it about?"

"I don't remember now," Dana murmured, lying down again.

But she *did* remember.

The feeling of someone—some presence—hovering over her.

The pressure on her throat.

The sharp stab of pain.

Dana reached up and touched her neck.

Her fingers quickly found the spot. A tiny bump on the smooth skin. A mosquito bite?

Yes. Of course.

A mosquito bite.

"Hey, there you are," Mickey declared as Dana wandered into the clearing the next morning. "I thought you'd never get up."

Dana stifled a moan. Her head ached. She felt shaky and tired.

"Dana! Mickey!" Marla cried as she rushed by. "We're going in ten minutes."

"Going where?" Dana asked.

"The hike," Marla called back over her shoulder. "Come on, you guys, get moving. It's a tradition!"

Dana moaned again.

"Whoa, you look *terrible*," Mickey remarked, putting his arm around Dana's shoulders.

"Thanks a lot." Dana sank down onto a log and sighed.

Marla hurried around, urging everybody to hurry up. Kids were taking down their tents, or stuffing plastic bottles of water and soda into their backpacks. Nothing remained of the morning campfire but a bed of dirt-covered ashes.

"Here—I saved you part of my breakfast." Mickey shoved a small paper plate under Dana's nose.

Dana glanced down at the small pile of scrambled eggs and almost gagged. "Thanks, but I don't think I can eat those," she murmured. "Not right now."

"Oh. Well, they're probably cold anyway." Mickey dumped the plate into a plastic garbage bag. "How about a granola bar?"

Dana shook her head.

"Some marshmallows?" he suggested. "I think there's a bag left over."

"Nothing. Really, I'm not hungry," Dana told him.

Mickey frowned. "Are you sick?"

"I'm not sure." Dana rested her elbows on her knees and propped her head in her hands. "I must be. I feel awful."

"Hey, you guys, how come you're just sitting here?" Deirdre dropped her backpack on the ground and knelt down to retie a shoelace.

"Dana feels sick," Mickey announced.

"Really?" Deirdre glanced up, a concerned expression on her face. "What's wrong?"

Dana shrugged. "I don't know. I just feel so weak. Maybe I caught a virus or something."

Is that why I had that nightmare? she wondered. People have weird dreams when they're sick.

"What about the hike?" Mickey asked.

Dana sighed. "I don't exactly feel like hiking."

"Do you want to go home?" Deirdre asked.

"No way," Dana replied. "I'll probably feel better in a little while. I just didn't sleep well. You guys go ahead. I'll wait here and take a nap."

"Are you sure?" Deirdre asked.

"Definitely." Dana glanced around. Marla had managed to gather the rest of the seniors at the edge of the clearing. "Hurry. They're leaving," she said, motioning toward the others.

Mickey leaned over and kissed her on the lips. "See you later," he murmured.

Dana kissed him back. As she pulled away, she noticed Deirdre watching them. Her sister glanced away quickly, but not quickly enough to hide the wishful expression in her eyes.

Oh, no, Dana thought.

Does Deirdre have a crush on Mickey? Is that why she blushes and stammers whenever she's near him? Is that why she gives me weird looks every time he kisses me?

Oh, wow.

I can't believe it! Does Deirdre really think Mickey would ever break up with me to go out with her?

Mickey and Deirdre hoisted their backpacks and joined the stream of kids heading into the woods.

Dana frowned. Poor Deirdre. She really shouldn't

try to compete with me. Especially when it comes to guys.

And what about Jon Milano? Dana wondered, watching them disappear into the trees. The two of them looked pretty cozy last night. I couldn't believe it when Deirdre wandered off with him, right after she nearly burned to death.

So why does she want Mickey, too? Is she just jealous of me? She has always wanted to be more like me. I know that. Now, suddenly, she wants my boyfriend, too?

Dana slid off the log and leaned against it.

The clearing stood silent now. Everyone had left.

Dana tilted her head back. The morning sun warmed her face and made her feel drowsy. Her tent was still up. Maybe she'd crawl back into it and sleep until everybody came back.

No, she decided. I'm comfortable here. It's nice in the fresh air.

Dana scooted lower until she could rest her head against the log.

As her eyes started to drift shut, a loud crack suddenly echoed through the clearing.

Dana bolted up, her heart racing.

Footsteps sounded behind her.

"Oh," a soft voice declared. "You're alone."

Dana spun around. And gasped. "Clark—what are you *doing* here?"

He didn't reply. He moved toward her quickly. "You're all alone," he repeated softly.

Chapter Thirteen

Deirdre Vanishes

"Clark—stop! You're scaring me!" Dana edged back. "What are you doing here? Why aren't you on the hike with everybody else?"

He hesitated. Just stared back at her with those cold, dark eyes.

"I got a late start. Didn't get to sleep until a couple of hours ago," he explained finally. "I just couldn't sleep at all. I was up all night."

He stood over her stiffly, hands shoved deep in the pockets of his black denim jeans.

Is he a vampire? Dana wondered.

Can the rumors about him be true?

Keep him talking, she decided. Keep him talking—and get ready to run.

She took a deep breath. A cool morning breeze

fluttered her hair. She brushed it off her forehead. "Clark, I'm surprised you came on the overnight trip since Debra didn't come." Her voice came out tight, shrill.

He shrugged, his eyes unblinking, burning into hers. "I didn't really want to come by myself. But Debra insisted. You know Debra. She made me come so I could tell her all about it later."

"Where is she? Is she sick?" Dana demanded.

"No. Not sick. Just really tired."

Clark gazed at her. "Like you."

Dana felt a shiver run down her back. "How do you know I'm tired?"

"Because you look it." Clark gave her a thin smile. "You didn't sleep well, either, did you? Is Danielle keeping you awake?"

"Huh?" she asked, startled. "*Danielle?* What on earth do you mean?"

"I figured you might be having bad dreams. You know. Since you were the one who found her," Clark explained. "Like last night. Were you having a nightmare about Danielle?"

"No. I wasn't dreaming about Danielle." Dana narrowed her eyes at him. Her heart suddenly pounded.

"What about you?" she asked. "Have you been dreaming about Danielle?

He didn't answer.

"Do you think they'll ever find out what happened?" Clark asked finally.

"I . . . I don't know."

"You've heard the 'Vampire Murder' stories on the news, haven't you?" he asked, his dark eyes flashing. "They say it's a psycho who kills like a vampire."

"I know," Dana replied. She shivered. Why does he sound so excited?

"Some people even believe there's a real vampire," Clark added, taking a few steps closer. "A real vampire in Shadyside. What do you think?"

Dana felt her whole body tense. "I don't know," she choked out. "I don't know what to think. Look—are you going on the hike? You'd better hurry up or everybody will be miles ahead of you."

Clark didn't move. His icy dark eyes remained locked on Dana.

His mouth opened slowly—and she expected long fangs to slide down.

"Guess I'd better go," he said finally. He turned and began to stride slowly away. After a few steps, he turned back to her, a strange frown on his face. "Get some rest, Dana. You look really. . . pale."

Dana let her breath out as Clark crossed the clearing and started onto the trail. His black hair, black jeans, and black T-shirt blended with the shadows.

Finally, he disappeared into the woods.

Count Clarkula, she thought.

Count Clarkula. . . Count Clarkula. . .

The nickname kept ringing in her ears.

Dana realized she was shivering and couldn't stop.

Was he trying to frighten me?

Or was he trying to tell me the truth?

Was he trying to *confess*?

"Hey, Sleeping Beauty! Come on—rise and shine!" a voice called out.

Dana came awake with a jerk.

Mickey stood above her, gazing down with a cheerful grin. A twig was caught in his blond hair, and burrs clung to his shirt like caterpillars.

Yawning, Dana slowly sat up against the log and glanced around.

Several seniors milled around the clearing, gathering up their camping gear. Others still stumbled in from the woods, looking tired and thirsty. Everyone seemed to be talking at once.

"Whoa." Dana yawned again. She stretched. "I was *unconscious*! I was really asleep. I didn't even hear you guys come back."

"No kidding." Mickey dropped onto the log and slung an arm around her shoulder. "I was going to slosh some water on you, but I decided I'd rather live."

Dana elbowed him in the ribs. "Good choice."

Mickey laughed. "How do you feel?"

"I'm not sure. Better, I think," Dana replied. She tilted her head back and forth. Her neck felt a little stiff from sleeping against the log.

But she definitely felt stronger.

"How was the hike?" she asked Mickey.

"Long and hot," he declared. "I'm ready for something ice-cold to drink. I'm starved, too. What do you say? How about Mickey D's?"

"Sure. I just want to go home and shower first," Dana told him. She stood up. "Hey, where's Deirdre? I thought she was walking with you."

"Only for a while," Mickey replied. "I went ahead with some other guys."

Dana glanced around the clearing again. Kids were gathering up trash and sleeping bags. Others called out good-byes and headed toward the flat grassy area where they had parked their cars.

A couple of kids stumbled in from off the trail, sweaty and tired. Behind them, Dana saw Anita Black.

Then Jon Milano.

I bet Deirdre is with Jon, Dana thought.

But Deirdre didn't emerge.

"Where could she be?" Dana wondered. She glanced around the clearing to where Deirdre's tent had been. The tent was packed away. Jennifer knelt in the dirt, stuffing a sweatshirt into her backpack.

"Jennifer?" Dana called, hurrying over with Mickey. "Have you seen Deirdre? Is she with Trisha?"

"Trisha left," Jennifer told her. "Why? You mean Deirdre isn't back yet?"

"No." A chill tightened the back of Dana's neck. "What could have happened to her?"

"Relax," Mickey told her. "She probably just finished early and caught a ride with somebody else."

Dana shook her head. "No way. She wouldn't leave without telling me."

"Then she must still be hiking the trail," Mickey declared.

"I don't think so," Jennifer said slowly. "I think everyone is back."

"Come on, you can't be sure," Mickey argued.

"Deirdre isn't crazy about the woods. She definitely wouldn't hang out there by herself," Dana told him. She bit her lip tensely. "I have to go look for her."

"Oh, come on," Mickey protested. "She's okay. She's a big girl, Dana."

Dana scowled at him. What's his problem? she wondered. It's like he doesn't want me to go.

"If it's so much trouble, you don't have to come," Dana snapped.

As she started toward the trail, Clark Dickson stumbled in from the woods. He was flushed and breathless.

Dana stared at him, horrified.

Twin trails of bright red blood flowed down from his lower lip. Two thick, glistening drops hung from his chin for a second, then dripped off onto his black T-shirt.

As Clark gazed at Dana, his lips parted. A froth of pink bubbles appeared.

His tongue swept across his lip, sucking the blood into his mouth.

Chapter Fourteen

Deirdre is Dead

As Dana gaped at Clark, a dozen frightening images flew through her mind.

Danielle on the gym floor . . . Clark dressed as a vampire at Trisha Conrad's party last spring . . . Clark poking his head last night into Dana's tent . . . moving so stealthily up to her this morning . . .

Deirdre . . . Deirdre alone, somewhere in the woods . . .

The blood . . . the blood . . .

Is that my sister's blood on Clark's lips?

Dana shook away the terrifying images. "What did you do to Deirdre?" she shrieked, rushing to him. "Where is she? Where?"

"Let me . . . catch my breath?" Clark bent over,

breathing heavily. Drops of blood spattered onto the dirt at his feet.

Finally, he turned to Dana and Mickey. "I . . . I ran from a skunk," he declared. "I smacked my face right into a low tree branch. Oww. My lip is really cut."

Dana eyed him warily. "But where is Deirdre?"

"Huh? What about her?" Clark mopped at his cut lip.

"Where *is* she?" Dana demanded shrilly.

"I don't know." Clark straightened up. "Why are you asking *me*?"

"Because she hasn't come back yet!"

"Oh." Clark frowned. "That's weird. I saw her way ahead of me when everybody started back. She should be here by now."

Dana stared at him. Is he telling the truth?

Or is he a lying murderer?

Fear rippled through her. Her heart raced. She had to find her sister.

Dana brushed past Clark and plunged into the woods. As she raced along the winding trail, she heard voices shouting after her.

"Dana, wait up!" Jennifer called.

"Where are you going?" Mickey cried.

"To find Deirdre!" Dana shouted over her shoulder. As she turned back, her shoe caught in a thick root that twisted across the trail. She stumbled and fell to her knees.

"Wait up!" Jennifer cried. She and Mickey ran

up as Dana scrambled to her feet. "I'm sure she's okay."

"No," Dana insisted, gasping for breath. "Something is wrong. I just know it. Did you see the blood on Clark's chin?"

"Huh? What's that got to do with anything?" Mickey asked. "Oh, wait—get serious. You don't really think he killed anybody, do you?"

"Even if he didn't, there *is* a killer running around, you know!" Dana cried. "And Deirdre is missing!"

Dana took off again, with Mickey and Jennifer following behind. Pounding along the trail, she tried to remember what her sister had been wearing that morning. That dark green sweatshirt? No, that was last night.

Blue and yellow, that's it, Dana remembered. A blue plaid flannel shirt over a yellow T-shirt. Good, at least the colors will be easy to spot.

Pausing for breath, Dana told Mickey and Jennifer about Deirdre's clothes. Then they hurried on. When the trail branched, Dana paused again.

"Left," Mickey told her. "The other way is a dead end. This way winds down to a creek."

"That's right," Jennifer agreed. "We all went wading on the way back."

Dana hurried on along the left branch of the trail, shouting Deirdre's name.

No response.

She kept turning her head, straining to see a

patch of blue or yellow somewhere in the thick green of the woods.

Where is she? Dana wondered frantically. What happened to her?

Please be okay. Please . . .

After a few minutes the trees thinned out on either side. The trail widened and began to slope down steeply. Digging her heels in to keep from falling, Dana hurried toward the splashing, gurgling sounds of the creek.

Halfway down the slope she finally spotted a bright patch of yellow. "Deirdre, is that you?" Dana cried. "Deirdre!"

No answer.

Dana plunged down, calling Deirdre's name. As she drew closer to the creek, she finally saw her sister.

Deirdre lay sprawled on her back next to the creek, her arms flung out from her sides. She'd rolled her jeans up and tied the plaid shirt around her waist. Her sneakers lay nearby, the white leather smeared with grass stains.

Deirdre's legs and bare feet angled toward the trail. Her head rested on the ground inches from the creek, and her blond hair swayed like seaweed as the water drifted around it.

"Deirdre!" Dana shouted. "Deirdre!"

She stumbled onto the flat ground and raced to her sister's side.

Mickey and Jennifer ran up behind her.

Dana frantically grabbed her sister's arm.

"Oh, no!" she gasped.

The skin . . . so cold. So cold!

And her face so pale, as if bleached of color.

"She's dead!" Dana screamed. "She's *dead*!"

Chapter Fifteen

The Vampire's Twin Victims

A sob rose in Dana's throat as she clutched Deirdre's arm.

She's dead. My sister is dead!

"Wait, look!" Jennifer cried. "She's breathing, Dana—look!"

Dana stared, her heart suddenly racing with hope. Through a blur of tears, she saw her sister's chest slowly rising and falling. "Deirdre!"

Deirdre's eyelids fluttered. She moaned softly and opened her eyes. "Huh? My hair. It's all wet," she murmured. She lifted her head and gazed around.

Dana and Mickey helped Deirdre sit up. "Your hair was in the creek," Dana explained. "Are you okay? What happened?"

"I'm not sure." Deirdre tilted her head and

squeezed the water out of her hair. Then she groggily gazed around again. "I remember taking my shoes off so I could go wading."

"How come you were by yourself?" Dana asked.

"I wasn't. I mean, there were a bunch of other kids on the trail behind me," Deirdre told her. "I thought they were coming down here, too. I guess they didn't see me or something."

"So what happened?" Dana repeated anxiously. "Try to remember."

"I was almost at the water and then . . ." Deirdre frowned. "It got very cloudy. Very dark."

"Huh? Dark? What do you mean?" Jennifer demanded.

Deirdre shrugged. "Things just got cloudy. Like I was in the middle of a really thick fog. And I couldn't breathe right. I guess I fainted or something."

Dana frowned. "Were you feeling sick? I mean, maybe the burns from last night . . ."

Deirdre glanced down at the gauze on her arm. "I don't think so," she said. "It hasn't hurt since last night."

Dana pictured Clark. "Are you sure you were alone? Did you see anybody before you fainted?"

"No. I heard people, but . . . !"

"A bee stung me!" Deirdre exclaimed. "Now I remember. When I was walking to the water, I heard a buzz. Then I felt a sharp sting."

"And you fainted from a bee sting?" Mickey asked skeptically.

Deirdre nodded. "I'm allergic to bees. That's why I couldn't breathe very well. It makes my windpipe close up or something."

As she spoke, Deirdre tugged her T-shirt away from her neck.

Dana leaned close and stared at her sister's throat.

Two tiny red dots marked the pale skin.

A chill ran up Dana's spine.

She lifted her hand to her own throat and brushed her fingertips across the small bump.

It's in the same place as Deirdre's, she thought.

Deirdre got stung by a bee.

But what about me? Was it a mosquito bite?

Or something else?

"I'm a total mess," Deirdre declared as she and Dana climbed the stairs to their bedroom later. "I can't wait to take a shower."

"Yeah." Dana dropped her backback onto the floor with a thud. I'm so tired, she thought. It's not normal. "Deirdre?"

"What?"

Dana crossed to the bed and slumped down on it. "Did you hear me scream last night?"

"Your nightmare, you mean?" Deirdre laughed as she peeled off her dirty jeans and T-shirt. "Everybody heard it."

"I'm not sure it was a nightmare."

"What do you mean?"

"Look." Dana pulled her sweatshirt away from her neck.

Deirdre shrugged on her fuzzy blue bathrobe and came over to the bed. She bent down and peered at Dana's throat. "What is it? A mosquito bite?"

"I don't think so," Dana replied. "It doesn't itch. But it's definitely a bite. The question is, what kind?"

"Huh?" Deirdre straightened up, a startled expression on her face.

"It sounds nuts, but. . ." Dana took a deep breath and told Deirdre about the presence she'd felt in her tent the night before.

About Clark, appearing just a few seconds later.

About how tired she felt.

How *drained*.

"Just like Debra, remember?" she said. "Ever since she's been seeing Clark, she's like a zombie. And this morning, before Clark went on the hike, he was talking about Danielle's blood. You should have seen his face. He. . . he was so *excited*!"

"That poem," Deirdre murmured. "'Your blood gives life. . .'" She broke off, jumping, as the telephone rang loudly.

Dana leaned over and picked it up. "Hello?"

A low, breathless voice came over the line. "I said you were next. Do you believe me now?"

PART FOUR

Chapter Sixteen

Leftovers

The final bell rang. Before it even finished, the handful of students had already hustled out the door.

Carla Sanders, the Shadyside High home economics teacher, heaved a sigh as she gazed around the empty classroom.

Why am I even teaching this course? she wondered. Hardly anyone wants to take it these days, not even girls. They probably think it's still just baking cupcakes and chocolate pudding, and sewing potholders.

She threaded her way through the desks to the back half of the room, where the ovens and cooktops were set up. Last week's assignment had been to create a nutritional dinner menu that also tasted good.

Today, they had cooked it. The kids had eaten everything in sight, but the smell of food still lingered in the air.

Carla flipped on the exhaust fans, then sponged down the counters again. School was over for the day, and she walked along the row of ovens, checking to make sure they'd all been turned off.

As she turned the fans off, she spotted a tray sitting on one of the desks. Deduct one point, she thought.

She left the kitchen area and picked up the tray, which was covered with bran muffin crumbs.

She turned back toward the kitchen and bumped against another desk.

The tray slipped from her hand and clattered to the floor.

Carla stared down at the scattered crumbs. She'd have to clean them up.

Deduct another point.

She stooped down for the tray. As she straightened up, she suddenly sensed that she was no longer alone.

A student stood across the classroom from her.

"You gave me a scare," she declared. "I didn't hear you come in."

"I'm sorry."

"Well, can I help you?" Carla asked. She raised the tray.

"I think so."

Carla frowned. "You—You're not in my Home Economics class, are you?"

"No. I came in for extra credit," the student replied, moving closer. "I'm working on my own project."

"I'm not sure I understand what you mean. You can't get extra credit if you're not taking the course," Carla said.

"Please." The student came closer. "I'm really hungry."

"Well, I'm sorry, but there's no food left." Carla gestured at the scattered crumbs. "That's the last of it, I'm afraid."

The student gazed at the crumbs for a second, then at Carla.

Carla suddenly realized how quiet everything had become. There must be students around someplace, either going to play rehearsal or to club meetings.

But the home economics room sat by itself at the end of a short hallway. The closest classroom was around the corner, and it was used as a study hall. With school over for the day, it would be empty.

The student took another step closer.

Then another.

Carla felt the hair prickle on her arms. This kid made her nervous and she didn't like it.

She slapped the tray onto a desktop and put

on her teacher's voice. "I don't think you were paying attention. There's nothing here for you. You'll have to leave. Do you hear me? You can't come in here and—"

The student's hand shot out.

Strong fingers dug into Carla's neck, choking off her words. The other hand clamped across her mouth and nose.

The student's mouth dropped open. A pair of sharp, white fangs slid down.

Carla's eyes widened in shock and terror.

She twisted and struggled, trying to break free.

But the hand clutching her throat slid around and grabbed the back of her neck, holding her tight.

Tighter . . . tighter . . .

Pain throbbed down her body.

The dagger-like fangs glistened.

The student's face drew closer.

Became a blur.

Carla felt a sharp sting on the side of her throat.

She tried to cry out. Tried to scream . . .

But a thick fog wrapped around her. Choked her . . .

Blinded her . . .

She felt herself slump. Suddenly felt so weak . . .

Felt something warm and wet dribbling down her throat.

Blood?

My blood?

Noooooooo.

As the fog swirled around her, darkening, darkening . . . she heard wet, gurgling sounds.

Lapping. Swallowing. Lapping.

The fog closed in completely.

Then she felt nothing.

She didn't hear the lapping sound as it continued for a few moments.

Or the silence when the meal was over.

Chapter Seventeen

Vampire and Victim Revealed!

D ana dropped a slice of raisin bread into the
toaster and sat down at the kitchen table.

The Wednesday morning newspaper
lay on the table, its bold, black headline
screaming up at her:

SECOND VAMPIRE MURDER!
Slain Teacher Drained of Blood

A color photo below the headlines showed
the front entrance of the high school, with
Ms. Sanders's body, wrapped in a blanket, being
carried out on a stretcher by grim-faced police
officers.

Dana flipped the newspaper over. She didn't

want to see the picture, and she didn't need to read the story.

She already knew what it would say.

Mickey told her all about it.

Mickey was the one who found Ms. Sanders.

He found her late Monday afternoon, stretched out on the floor of the home economics room. "Ice cold and stiff," he said. "White as chalk."

Of *course* she was white as chalk, Dana thought sadly.

All the blood was missing from her body.

She had been drained dry. Drained... just like poor Danielle Cortez.

The raisin toast popped up, but Dana changed her mind about eating it. The sweet aroma was making her sick. She didn't feel hungry anymore. She'd just have some juice.

As she stood at the counter pouring a glass of orange juice, Deirdre entered the kitchen. She wore a black skirt and a black, short-sleeved sweater.

Dana eyed the clock over the stove. Ten-thirty. School had been canceled for two days. "What are you up to? You look like you're going to a funeral."

"That's not till Friday, remember?" Deirdre reminded her. "Trisha's picking me up. She talked me into going to the mall. Thought it might take our minds off of things. But I doubt it."

Dana sipped some juice and set it down

quickly as her stomach began to churn. "Two funerals, and it's still September," she murmured in a choked whisper.

She suddenly remembered Trisha Conrad's ugly vision. The Doomed Class . . .

That's us. We're the Doomed Class.

"How's Mickey doing?" Deirdre asked.

"What do you mean?"

"Well, he found her body," Deirdre explained. "He must have been totally messed up. Did you talk to him? Is he okay?"

Dana shrugged. Mickey didn't act shocked. He wasn't the type, she guessed.

"What was he doing in the home economics room, anyway?" Deirdre demanded.

"How am I supposed to know?" Dana snapped. "I didn't ask him. Stop bugging me."

"Sorry!" Deirdre pulled a chair out. She sat down, then hopped up almost immediately. "I can't sit still. I'm so scared! I can't believe this is happening!"

"Me, either." Dana poured the juice down the sink. "I just wish the police would stop fooling around and arrest Clark. It's so obvious."

"But they questioned him again for hours," Deirdre reminded her. "The police know the rumors about Clark. If they believed they had any real evidence against him . . ." Her voice trailed off.

"Yeah, well, they didn't ask Clark the right questions," Dana declared. She put the glass in the dishwasher. "And they should look at his phone records or something."

"Maybe they did. I mean, we told them about the phone calls. We told them about the blood on his lips. We told them how he prowled around while we were all sleeping."

Deirdre shook her head. "Do you really think he's the murderer?" she asked.

"I don't know. Nobody knows anything, not even the police—except there's some psycho killer running around pretending to be a vampire!" Dana cried.

She touched her throat, rubbing the small bump with her thumb.

"How do you feel?" Deirdre asked her.

"Oh, great. I mean, the killer only took a tiny sip, right?" Dana replied sarcastically. Actually, she didn't feel so tired anymore.

I was lucky this time, she thought.

The doorbell rang.

"It's Trisha," Deirdre said. She hurried out of the kitchen.

Dana leaned against the counter. I almost wish they hadn't canceled school, she thought. It would take our minds off things, at least.

"Dana!" Deirdre called, her voice sharp with fear. "Come here, quick!"

Dana rushed into the hall.

Trisha stood just inside the front door. She looked beautiful, as usual.

But her mouth was open in a silent scream of horror.

And her brown eyes stared straight ahead. Blank. Unblinking.

Focusing on something no one else could see.

"Trisha!" Deirdre cried, shaking her friend's shoulder. "Please! Snap out of it!"

Trisha kept staring.

Finally a shudder passed through her. She took a sharp breath and blinked rapidly. Her eyes finally focused and she gazed back and forth at the twins.

"What was that all about?" Dana demanded. "Are you sick?"

"No, she had a vision! Didn't you, Trisha?" Deirdre asked.

Trisha nodded. "I really hate this!" she burst out. "These psychic flashes—why do I have to get them? I don't want to be psychic. It's just not fair!"

"What was it?" Deirdre asked. "What did you see?"

Trisha clasped her hands together and took a shaky breath. "I saw the two of you," she replied. "I couldn't tell which was which."

Dana exchanged a glance with her sister.

Deirdre's face had gone pale.

Dana felt a stab of nervousness. *I never really believed in Trisha's visions,* she thought.

But I never saw her actually have one.

"I probably shouldn't be telling you, but . . ." Trisha took another deep breath. "One of you was dead."

Deirdre gasped.

"And the other one . . ." Trisha paused, swallowing. "The other one was drinking her blood!"

Chapter Eighteen

Grabbed

Deirdre sat in Mr. Morley's social studies class on Thursday afternoon staring down at her notebook.

No notes. She hadn't taken any notes because she hadn't heard a word of Mr. Morley's lecture.

Instead, she kept thinking about Trisha's psychic flash. Hearing Trisha's bizarre, frightening words: "One of you was drinking the other one's blood."

Deirdre shivered, playing the scene over and over again in her mind. When Trisha told them about the vision, Dana pretended to laugh. But she didn't fool Deirdre.

Dana is scared because of that weird mark on her neck, Deirdre thought.

But she's feeling better. She's not as tired, and she isn't pale at all.

But what did Trisha's vision mean? That one of us sisters is going to die?

No.

That we're *all* going to die. We're doomed, Trisha said. She saw us rotting in our graves. The whole senior class.

A movement caught Deirdre's eye. She turned toward the door.

A bulky man was moving slowly down the hall. He wore a tan uniform with a badge on the shirt pocket.

And a gun at his waist.

The man turned his head from side to side as he walked. His gaze swept coolly over Deirdre's face. Then he moved out of sight.

Deirdre shivered again. They're all over the school, she thought. Private security guards, patrolling the halls with guns. Watching everybody with cold, suspicious eyes.

She knew the guards had been hired for everyone's protection. But they made the school feel like a prison. And they reminded everyone of what had happened.

Two people had been viciously murdered.

And the killer was still on the loose.

Deirdre glanced around the classroom. Most kids were still staring at the door where the guard had passed. But Mary O'Connor sat with her head down, gazing sadly at her desktop.

What is she thinking about? Deirdre wondered.

As Mr. Morley scrawled the homework assignment on the board, the bell rang. Deirdre didn't even bother to write the assignment down. She'd call someone tonight. She couldn't stand to spend a second longer in this school.

Anxious to get away, Deirdre shot out of the room—and crashed into Stacy Malcolm.

"Whoa!" Stacy staggered backward.

"Sorry." Deirdre stepped aside as kids from the class jostled her from behind. "I . . . I wasn't looking."

"No kidding." Stacy adjusted her hat, a soft, black felt one with a rainbow-ribboned band. "What's your rush, anyway?"

"I want to get out of here. Don't you?" Deirdre asked. "I mean, it's awful. How can we have a normal school day when two people have been murdered and there are guys with guns all over the place?"

"You mean the security guards? Guess what—they're not all guys," Stacy told her. "A woman guard checked out the bathroom while I was in there during fourth period. Freaked me out."

Mary O'Connor brushed past Deirdre on her way out the door. "Hi," she murmured. "Stacy, call me tonight, okay?"

"Sure." Stacy waited until Mary was out of earshot. "She's really upset about Gary," she told

Deirdre. "She's afraid he's going to break up with her—for Trisha."

"I know."

"Is he?" Stacy demanded. "What did Trisha tell you?"

"Nothing. Really." Deirdre paused as another security guard strode past. "Look, I'm going home," she declared. "I can't stand being here."

"But, Deirdre, you're forgetting," Stacy replied.

"Forgetting? Forgetting what?"

"Girls' basketball tryouts," Stacy said. "They're in the gym—in twenty minutes."

"Oh, yeah." Deirdre frowned. "Stacy, I really don't think I should. I told you I have to keep my grades up. Besides, how can anybody even think about sports after what's happened?"

Stacy rolled her eyes. "What are we supposed to do—crawl under a rock? Look, maybe if you concentrate on something else, you'll stop feeling so scared all the time."

"Maybe you're right," Deirdre admitted. "But I haven't played in a long time."

"Big deal. I'll bet you're still as good," Stacy argued. "You have talent. And you know it."

Deirdre hesitated.

"Come on, Deirdre, the team needs you. Stop making up excuses."

Deirdre couldn't help smiling. Stacy could really be pushy when she wanted something. "Okay," she agreed. "But if I make the team and my grades start to slide, *promise* you will let me quit without an argument."

"Deal. But it's going to be great, you'll see." Stacy glanced at her watch. "Come on, let's get to the gym."

"I'll meet you there," Deirdre told her. "I have to go to my locker first."

Staring into her locker, Deirdre tried to remember what she needed for homework. Her mind was totally blank. She finally stuffed everything into her backpack, just in case. Then she slammed the locker shut and started toward the gym.

Maybe Stacy is right, she thought as she passed another security guard. Playing basketball might help me take my mind off the murders. At least it'll make me tired, and maybe I'll sleep better.

As she drew closer to the gym, Deirdre began remembering some of the games she'd played with the team in the past. She wasn't as tall as a lot of the other players, but she was a good passer and had a really sharp shooting eye.

She pictured herself ducking and pivoting, putting herself in the perfect position to catch the ball, then shooting it crosscourt to a teammate.

Maybe Stacy was right, she thought. This is a good idea. She picked up her pace and rounded the corner to the gym.

She passed the empty band room.

The Thirst

Hands grabbed her from behind. Fingers covered her eyes, shutting out the light.

Deirdre opened her mouth in a scream of terror.

Chapter Nineteen

Another Victim?

"**W**hoa, wait! Shh!" a voice pleaded as Deirdre started to scream again. "Shh, it's me—Jon!"

"Jon!" Deirdre spun around. "What are you doing?" she shouted.

"Shh!" Jon glanced over his shoulder. "You want every guard in the place to start shooting?"

Deirdre took a deep breath. Her heart raced.

Jon watched her, an amused expression on his lean face.

"How could you sneak up on me like that?" Deirdre demanded.

"Easy. You were off in your own little world," he told her.

"You know what I mean," she declared. "Everybody is scared to death around here, in case you didn't notice."

"Okay, okay." Jon held up his hands. "I'm sorry. Really. I wasn't thinking. I . . . was just happy to see you."

Deirdre let her breath out slowly. "Where did you come from, anyway?" she asked, feeling calmer.

He pointed down the hall. "I chased after you. You didn't even hear me calling you."

"I . . . was thinking about things," she replied.

"I haven't really had a chance to talk to you since that teacher got killed," Jon said. "It's so scary. Have you heard anything? I mean, do the police have any ideas?"

"I don't know. No one wants to talk about it," Deirdre declared. "It's so ghastly. Some sick killer acting like a vampire."

"Maybe it's a *real* vampire," Jon murmured. "I never believed in vampires before. But . . ."

Deirdre shrugged. "Some kids believe there's a real vampire. But that's just so crazy, don't you think?"

Jon started to say something. Then he stopped suddenly and leaned close—and kissed her on the mouth.

Deirdre was so startled, she almost pulled away. But his lips felt so warm. So good.

She kissed him back.

"Listen, I have to go," he told her. "Maybe I'll catch up with you this weekend."

He gave her a quick wave and trotted around the corner.

Deirdre sighed and hurried on to the gym. She felt let down. And annoyed. Why should he have to "catch up" with me? she wondered. Why doesn't he just ask me out?

As she entered the gym, the echo of thumping basketballs and squeaking sneakers chased Jon from her mind. Everybody was already out on the floor, practicing jump shots, passing the ball around.

Deirdre hurried to the locker room. She shoved open the door. As the door swung shut behind her, she froze.

A soft black hat lay upside down at the end of the first row of lockers.

Stacy's hat, with the rainbow-ribbon band.

Stacy lay next to it, facedown on the tile floor.

Chapter Twenty

A Strange Smile

"**N**oooo!" Deirdre wailed. "Oh, Stacy, nooo!"

Her heart stopped.

It's happened again! she thought.

Terrified and blinded with tears, she swung around and fumbled for the door handle.

"Deirdre! What's wrong?"

Deirdre spun back, gasping.

Stacy climbed to her feet.

"Stacy!" Deirdre dropped her bookbag and fell against the door. "You're okay?"

"You practically gave me a heart attack, screaming like that," Stacy sighed. "I dropped a contact. I nearly stepped on it." She raised the palm of her hand carefully.

"I saw you lying there and I thought . . ." Deirdre took a shuddering breath. "I thought . . ."

125

Stacy gave her a hug. "Thanks for worrying about me. But I'm fine. Nothing bad happened."

Not this time, Deirdre thought. She took a deep breath. "Aren't you scared, Stacy?

"Sure I am, but. . ." Stacy hesitated for a second, then tossed her head. "Let's not talk about it. Come on and change your clothes. Let's get out on the floor."

"Looking good, Deirdre!" Stacy shouted as Deirdre ducked away from Jennifer and shot a three-pointer from the top of the key.

"Nice shot," an unfamiliar voice called.

Deirdre turned and found Anita Black smiling at her. "Hey—you're trying out? That's great!" Deirdre exclaimed.

"I'm so tall, everyone always tells me I should play basketball," Anita said, tossing her auburn ponytail over her shoulder. "So I thought I'd give it a try."

"I haven't really played in a while," Deirdre confessed. "And I feel a little rusty. Do you play center?"

"No. Forward," Anita replied.

"Well, all right!" Deirdre grabbed a ball. She and Anita moved down the court, dribbling, passing to each other.

"It must be hard transferring in your senior year," Deirdre said. "Do you know anyone at Shadyside?"

Anita heaved up a two-handed jump shot. Too

hard. It bounced off the glass. "Not really," she replied. "Well . . . I know Jon Milano. We . . . Actually, we used to go out."

"Really?" Deirdre stopped short and studied Anita.

"But that was sophomore year," Anita continued. "Jon and I . . . well . . . we don't really talk much anymore. Just say 'hi' when we pass each other in the hall. You know."

Deirdre nodded. She bounced the ball a few times. "He seems like an okay guy," she said, trying to keep her voice steady, trying not to sound too interested.

Anita smiled. "Yeah. He's okay. We just . . . weren't on the same wavelength."

Ms. Martin, the basketball coach, blew a whistle. She divided the girls into two teams. "I want to see you guys play all out," she instructed. "I know it's only the first practice. But let's see what you can do."

The teams went at it. The play was ragged. Sloppy. No one could shoot.

Deirdre let a pass dribble through her fingertips. She shook her head, scowling.

"You'll get the next one," Anita called.

Anita grabbed the ball away from Stacy. Stole it easily from her hands. She spun away, faked, and dribbled to the basket for an easy layup.

She's good, Deirdre thought. With those long, skinny legs, she looks like an ostrich when she runs. But she can really handle the ball.

A few seconds later Anita had the ball again. Jennifer Fear moved to the basket, waving frantically for the ball.

Anita pulled her arm back, preparing to heave it.

Deirdre dived forward, hoping to intercept.

"Ohhh." A groan escaped Deirdre's throat as the ball slammed hard into the pit of her stomach.

She saw red. Then black.

Can't breathe . . . can't breathe . . .

The ball had knocked her air out. Deirdre dropped to her knees. The gym walls spun around her.

"Are you okay?"

"Deirdre? Do you need help?"

Anita dropped down beside Deirdre. "I'm so sorry!" she cried. "I didn't see you. Really. I didn't mean—"

"Not . . . your . . . fault," Deirdre choked out.

Stacy and Jennifer helped her to the sideline. Coach Martin told her to sit and catch her breath until she felt like playing.

Deirdre leaned against the cool tile wall. Her stomach ached, but she was breathing normally now. She glanced up to the bleachers across the gym. A few kids had come to watch the tryouts.

Who was that figure in black in the top row? Clark?

Deirdre squinted into the bright light. Yes. It was Clark. Why is he here? she wondered. Clark isn't a basketball fan. He isn't in to any sports at all.

What is he doing here?

"Deirdre—feeling better?" Coach Martin asked. She handed Deirdre the ball. "Let's play a little one-on-one. Drive for a layup."

The coach motioned to Anita. "You guard her. Let's see you play the D."

Deirdre took the ball in. Dribbling softly, she backed over the line, then started her drive. Anita moved with her, her eyes narrowed in concentration.

Deirdre faked right. Moved left. But Anita didn't go for the fake. She stabbed at the ball with both hands, nearly stealing it from Deirdre.

Deirdre spun away. Started her drive to the basket.

She saw Anita's sneaker come up in front of her. Too late to stop.

"Noooo!" Deirdre gasped as she stumbled over the sneaker. The ball bounced away. Deirdre fell hard. Tried to stop. But skidded . . . skidded on her elbows and knees.

She heard the whistle blow. Heard stampeding sneakers as the girls hurried to surround her once again.

Gritting her teeth against the pain, Deirdre scrambled to her knees. Oh, wow, she thought. That really hurt.

And what was that expression on Anita's face? Was that a smile?

No.

No. Anita couldn't be smiling—*could* she?

Chapter Twenty-one

Accidents?

"**D**eirdre, you've got some bad floor burns." Coach Martin's voice burst into Deirdre's troubled thoughts.

Deirdre rubbed her elbow. Felt warm, wet blood. She had scraped all the skin off.

"Better hurry to the nurse's office," the coach instructed. "I think she's still there. Better get your knees bandaged too, Deirdre. You cut them up pretty good."

"I'll help her," Anita offered.

And before Deirdre realized what was happening, Anita had her arm around her waist and was leading her to the nurse. Repeating, "I'm sorry. I'm so sorry," all the way down the hall.

"Whoa!" Dana exclaimed when Deirdre entered

their bedroom later that afternoon. "What happened to your knees?"

"I fell during basketball tryouts." Deirdre dropped her backpack on the floor. She lifted her arms and stuck her elbows out. "My elbows got wrecked, too, thanks to Anita Black."

"Huh?"

"She tripped me," Deirdre declared. "It was an accident. But that girl is a major disaster area!"

"What do you mean?" Dana demanded.

"First she slams the ball into my stomach. Then we're playing one-on-one, and she sticks out her big foot and trips me."

"Weird," Dana muttered. "Is she some kind of competitive freak?"

"I don't think so," Deirdre replied. "I think maybe she's just a total klutz."

"She's so tall," Dana said, gazing at Deirdre's bandaged knees. "Like a giraffe. But she seems nice."

"Yeah," Deirdre agreed. "She must have said she was sorry at least a thousand times."

Dana eyed her intently. "Wasn't Anita the girl who pushed you into the fire?"

"She didn't push me," Deirdre replied. "She bumped me. Another accident."

Dana snickered. "This girl is bad luck. Hey—I almost forgot! Did you make the team?"

"Yes," Deirdre replied. "I played really well— until the accident. Anita made the team too.

Maybe she'll be less lethal when we're on the same side!"

They both laughed.

Deirdre shook her hair out. It was tangled and stiff with sweat. She hadn't even bothered to change into her regular clothes after she'd seen the nurse. I need a shower, she thought.

She started for the door. Her foot nudged a corner of her backpack.

The pack fell over and her clothes tumbled out.

As Deirdre kicked them aside, a folded-up sheet of paper slid out.

She picked it up and opened it.

An icy panic flooded through her as she read the scrawled words:

YOUR SISTER'S BLOOD WAS SO SWEET.
YOURS WILL BE EVEN SWEETER.

Chapter Twenty-two

Pursued in the Night

O n Saturday night Deirdre sat cross-legged on the floor in Jennifer's bedroom. Her gaze fell on her scraped knee. She had removed the bandage. But the knee was still red, with blood crusted around the edges.

YOUR SISTER'S BLOOD WAS SO SWEET.

YOURS WILL BE EVEN SWEETER.

Deirdre jumped as something bounced lightly off the top of her head and landed on the floor in front of her.

A kernel of popcorn.

She picked it up and popped it into her mouth.

"You *are* alive!" Stacy declared. She sat on the bed, leaning against the headboard. A big bowl of popcorn rested on top of her stretched-out legs. "Jennifer and I were starting to worry."

"Right," Jennifer agreed. She was curled up in a big armchair in the corner. "You've been sitting there like a statue all night, Deirdre."

"What were you thinking about?" Stacy asked.

The horrible message flashed through Deirdre's mind again.

She hadn't told anyone but Dana about the note. Why scare everybody else?

The killer is not after them, Deirdre thought.

He's after me.

"Earth to Deirdre," Stacy said. "What is on your mind?"

"Jon," Deirdre lied. Actually, if it weren't for the note, she probably *would* have been thinking about him. "He wasn't in school yesterday, and he didn't call. So obviously, we aren't going out this weekend."

"You should have called him," Jennifer scolded.

"I tried Information. His number is unlisted." Deirdre stretched her legs out, wincing a little.

"Your knees still hurt, huh?" Stacy asked.

Deirdre nodded. "Not too much, though."

"It's great that you made the team," Jennifer said.

"Yeah, and Anita, too. We needed a real power forward."

"She tripped you on purpose," Stacy blurted out. "I know she did."

"That's crazy," Deirdre replied heatedly. "She apologized a thousand times. Why did you say that?"

Stacy shrugged. "It looked deliberate to me. I don't trust her."

"You're wrong, Stacy," Jennifer chimed in. "Anita was nervous trying out, that's all. Anyway, we're all on the same team now."

Stacy made a face. "Guess who I saw on the way over here?"

"Who?" Deirdre asked.

"Trisha—with Gary Fresno," Stacy replied. "What a jerk. They were in her father's Mercedes. They stopped ahead of me at a light, and I had to sit there and watch them make out until the light turned green."

Deirdre frowned. "Trisha is not a jerk."

"What do you call someone who goes out with somebody else's boyfriend?" Stacy demanded. "Mary is crazy about Gary, and Trisha knows it."

"So? Maybe Trisha is crazy about him, too," Deirdre argued. "What's she supposed to do?"

"I can't believe you're sticking up for her," Stacy exclaimed.

"Hey, guys, don't fight," Jennifer said.

Deirdre ignored her. "I'm just saying that Gary is the jerk—not Trisha," she told Stacy. "He's the one who's going out with two people at the same time."

"Yeah, because Trisha came on to him."

"I don't believe this." Deirdre leaped to her feet. "Trisha is your friend. How can you trash her like that?"

"Because Mary is my friend too. And because Trisha is hurting Mary. Because she's wrong," Stacy declared heatedly. "And you know it."

"This is ridiculous." Deirdre grabbed her jacket from the bed and stomped to the door.

"Where are you going?" Jennifer asked.

Deirdre opened the door. "Home."

"Deirdre, wait!" Jennifer cried. "You can't—"

Deirdre slammed the door, shutting out Jennifer's and Stacy's words. She trotted down the stairs and hurried outside, shrugging on her jacket as she reached the sidewalk.

A fog had rolled in, turning the street lights hazy. The tree trunks were black with moisture, and water dripped from the leaves.

Deirdre shivered as she hurried along the sidewalk. Drops of water splashed onto her head and rolled down her face and neck. She skidded on some wet leaves plastered across the sidewalk and almost fell.

Stupid, she told herself as she caught her balance. Why did you pick a fight with Stacy? She was only sticking up for Mary.

Deirdre jammed her hands into her jacket pockets, hunching her shoulders against the chill. She glanced around.

The street is so empty, she thought.

No one is out here but me.

She felt a quiver of fear.

Why did I come out here alone?

She swallowed nervously. Should I go back? No. I'm closer to home already.

Deirdre hurried on. Mist beaded on her eyelashes, then rolled down her cheeks.

Tires hissed on the wet street behind her. She glanced over her shoulder.

A car rolled down the street, its headlights glowing through the fog.

The car drew closer. Came alongside her.

Deirdre glanced at it out of the corner of her eye.

A small, silver sports car.

Was it a Porsche? It was kind of beat up.

Its engine rumbled.

Deirdre turned her eyes forward and walked faster.

Pass me, she thought. Go on. Drive by.

But the car slowed. Kept pace with her.

Deirdre's heart fluttered.

She was alone, and she didn't see any other cars.

Maybe the driver just wants directions, she told herself. She glanced over, but a film of fog covered the passenger window. She couldn't see inside.

Her heart began to thud. A wave of fear swept over her.

If the driver wanted directions, he would have asked by now.

She walked on, taking long strides.

The car stayed by her side.

She picked up her pace, walking rapidly, head bent against the mist.

The car stayed with her.

Then it squealed to a halt beside her.

Deirdre's heart pounded with terror.

"What do you want?" she cried. "What do you want?"

Chapter Twenty-three

Kidnapped?

The driver's door clicked.

The dome light came on. In its dim, misty glow, Deirdre saw the dark silhouette of the driver.

She froze, her heart banging hard inside her chest.

The driver's door began to open, squeaking loudly.

"Deirdre—it's *you*!" a voice called.

Jon?

"I *thought* it was you," he called out to her. "But I wasn't sure."

"You—you scared me to death!" she gasped in a hoarse whisper.

"Oh. Sorry," he replied. "It was so foggy. I couldn't see if it was you. Come on. Get in." He motioned to her. "Didn't I say I might catch up with you this weekend? Well, here I am!"

Forcing her heartbeat to return to normal, Deirdre took a deep breath and then slid into the small car beside him.

"What are you doing out here, anyway?" he asked.

"I had an argument with . . . oh, never mind," Deirdre said. "It's dumb." A chill shook her. She hugged herself.

"I'll turn up the heater," Jon said. "Are you hungry? We could grab something at the mall. I'm starving."

"That sounds great," she agreed. She sighed as the warm air floated up over her.

"Do you like the car?" he asked, revving the motor till it roared.

"Are you kidding? It's awesome." Deirdre held her hands out in front of the heating vent. "Are you rich or something? How'd you get a Porsche?"

He chuckled. "It was a total wreck when I bought it. I fixed it up myself. It took forever!"

Deirdre couldn't stop shivering. Was it the cold or the fog? Or the scare Jon had accidentally given her?

"Still cold?" Jon pulled her to him. His eyes lit up as he bent his face close to hers.

He kissed her.

Deirdre kissed him back, her heart pounding.

Jon suddenly pulled away and gazed at her face. With a sigh, he brushed his fingertip over the mole on her cheek. He kissed it softly, then sat up straight and took hold of the steering wheel. "Ready to go?"

Without waiting for an answer, he slammed the stick into first and stepped on the gas. The tires squealed and the car shot forward.

Deirdre reached for her seat belt.

"Hey, don't worry," Jon told her. "I can handle this car with my eyes closed."

"Don't try it," she joked. She ran her hand along the leather dashboard. "I guess you took auto mechanics in your last school, huh?" she asked, buckling the seat belt.

"No way. That school had lots of things happening, but mechanics wasn't one of them."

Deirdre glanced at him. She could see his bitter expression in the eerie, greenish glow of the dashboard lights.

He'd some kind of trouble at his last school, she remembered. She wondered what it was, but decided not to ask.

"So how did you learn about cars? Did you work at a garage or something?" she asked.

He shook his head. "I taught myself. It's easy."

"So you're a mechanical genius?" Deirdre snickered. "Do you make straight A's, too?"

"Yeah, except for . . ." Jon broke off. "Hey. You're teasing me, right?"

"A little," Deirdre admitted.

Jon grew quiet. He reached out and flipped on the radio. As the pounding beat of a rap song blared from the speakers, he zoomed dangerously close to the rear of another car.

Deirdre pressed back against the seat.

At the last second Jon jerked the wheel to the left and zipped around the other car. Its driver honked angrily, but the sound faded fast as Jon sped ahead.

Deirdre let her breath out, then sucked it in again as Jon raced through an intersection on the yellow light.

"Don't tell me," she said. "You're trying out for the Waynesbridge Speedway."

Jon turned the music down and took hold of her hand. "Relax," he murmured. "Didn't I say you were safe with me?"

He let go of her hand to hold the wheel again. But Deirdre could still feel the pressure from his fingers. She settled back in the seat and tried to relax.

After a moment she realized something. They'd been driving for too long. They should have reached Division Street by now.

Where are we? she wondered.

Deirdre rubbed the fog from her window and peered outside.

No houses or other buildings. No traffic lights. No cross streets. She saw only endless, dark fields.

A sign flashed by on her right, too fast for her to read. But it didn't matter—she'd seen plenty of signs like that before.

"Wait—why are we on the highway?" Deirdre demanded shrilly. "Jon—where are you going? This isn't the way to the mall!"

Chapter Twenty-four

The Vampire Confesses

The car sped up.

"Jon, where are you going?" Deirdre demanded shrilly. "Stop! Where are you taking me?"

"Right there!" Jon pointed to the right, then jerked the wheel hard—and flew onto an exit ramp.

Ahead of them a traffic light changed to green. Jon swerved onto a side road and squealed to a halt on the grassy shoulder.

Deirdre let out her breath and glared at him. "Where are we?"

"I *thought* I was going to the mall," he replied.

"Huh? The mall?"

"I'm sorry. I didn't mean to get on the highway. I must have made a wrong turn. I'm new here, remember? I don't know my way around very well yet."

"Oh. Right. Of course." Deirdre blew out another breath. "Well, do you always drive like a crazed maniac?"

Jon laughed and pushed a strand of hair off her forehead. "Didn't you know? Maniac is my middle name."

Deirdre rolled her eyes.

"How come I get the feeling you don't trust me?" he teased. He cupped his hand on the back of her neck and squeezed gently.

Deirdre felt a tingle of pleasure.

Jon pulled her toward him and kissed her, hard. Harder.

"Maybe we should forget about the mall," he murmured softly, his lips pressed against her cheek.

"What do you mean?"

He pressed his forehead against her cheek. "I kind of like it right here," he breathed.

Whoa, Deirdre thought. He's exciting and sexy, but it's way too soon.

"What do you say?" Jon started to kiss her again.

She pulled back. "I'm really hungry. Come on. I'll give you directions to the mall."

Jon sighed, disappointed. But he turned the car around and drove north toward Division Street.

The Burger Barn was jammed with Shadyside High students. Deirdre spotted Dana and Mickey sitting in a booth near the back. Dana caught her eye and waved her over.

"There's my sister," Deirdre said to Jon. "Why don't you find us a table? If the waiter comes, order me a tuna-fish pita and a Coke."

"Huh?" He narrowed his eyes at her. "You come to the Burger Barn for *tuna-fish*?"

She laughed. "Don't look at me like that. It's not so weird. I've been trying to cut down on red meat."

As she walked toward Dana's booth, Deirdre caught snatches of conversation. "My mom thinks they should close the school until they catch the killer," a guy declared.

"Yeah, my parents are freaked out, too," someone agreed.

Everyone is talking about the murders, Deirdre thought.

Everyone is scared.

Dana grinned as Deirdre approached her booth. "You didn't tell me you were going out with Jon."

"I didn't know I was." Deirdre smiled at Mickey. "Hey, Mickey."

Mickey nodded. He had hamburger juice running down his chin.

"Look at this geek. Can't take him anywhere," Dana sighed.

Deirdre glanced over her shoulder. Jon sat in a booth on the far side of the restaurant, talking to a waiter. "I'd better go," she said. "Catch you guys later."

"Have fun!" Dana told her slyly.

As Deirdre threaded her way through the tables, she spotted Kenny and his girlfriend, Jade. Josh sat with them.

Trisha sat in a booth with Gary. Deirdre tried to catch Trisha's eye, but her friend didn't notice. She and Gary were totally focused on each other.

Deirdre was halfway across the restaurant when a hand reached out from a booth and grabbed her wrist.

She cried out as the fingers tightened and the hand pulled her close.

"Hey—!" Deirdre turned to see Clark grinning at her. "Let go! Clark!"

He sat by himself in a small booth. He wore a black turtleneck over black denim jeans. His dark eyes gleamed under the bright ceiling lights.

He slowly loosened his grip on her wrist. "Just wanted to say hi," he said.

"Well, hi," Deirdre replied, annoyed. "You didn't have to grab me, Clark. I—"

"Did you get my note?" he whispered, his eyes burning intently into hers.

Deirdre gasped. "Huh? Did you—? Are you the one—?"

"Did you get it? Did you get my note?" Clark repeated eagerly.

Chapter Twenty-five

Lap ... Lap ... Lap ...

H e stared up at her, his hand still wrapped around her wrist. A strange smile played over his lips.

"You?" Deirdre gasped.

Clark nodded. "I wrote to congratulate you. On making the basketball team. I watched your try-out. You were terrific, Deirdre."

Her mouth dropped open. What was he saying? She couldn't follow.

"I'm writing an article," Clark continued. "Do you believe they made me a sports reporter on the newspaper?"

"No," Deirdre murmured. "So the note you wrote to me—"

"I just wanted to say, 'Way to go!'" Clark declared.

"And the other note . . . ?" Deirdre demanded, her mind whirling.

Clark's dark eyes narrowed. "What other note? I only sent one."

Is he telling the truth? Deirdre wondered, studying his dark features, his glowing, black eyes. Or is he teasing me? Playing some kind of cold, cruel joke?

Why would Clark send me a note congratulating me for making the team? That's too weird. Too weird to believe . . .

I think he's trying to frighten me.

And I think it's working.

She uttered a goodbye. Pulled her wrist free. And hurried to join Jon.

"What's going on?" he demanded as she slid into the booth across from him.

"Do you know Clark?" she asked breathlessly. She pointed. "Have you met him?"

"Count Clarkula?" Jon snickered. "Yeah. He's in my gym class. Weird guy."

"Yes," Deirdre agreed. "Weird—and scary." And then she blurted out, "Do you believe in vampires, Jon? I mean, do you believe a vampire came into the school and murdered Danielle and Ms. Sanders?"

He stared across the table at her, thinking hard. "No," he replied finally. "I don't believe in vampires. And just because Clark dresses in black and acts weird—well . . . I don't think he's a vampire. I think he's just kind of sad. He's trying so hard to be different."

The waitress brought their food. Deirdre picked up the tuna-fish pita, but she didn't feel like eating. Her talk with Clark had tied her stomach in a knot.

"Anyway, Jon," she started. "Let's change the subject. Let's talk about . . . Jon?"

He was staring over her shoulder. He didn't seem to hear her.

"Jon? Who are you looking at?" she demanded shrilly.

"Nobody," he replied. "Just checking out the place." He lifted his double cheeseburger to his mouth.

Deirdre twisted around to see behind her. She saw Anita at a table with two other girls she didn't recognize.

Was Jon staring at Anita?

"I'm so excited about being back on the basketball team," she said, turning back to him. "Are you going to come to the games?"

"Yeah. Sure," he replied absently. He slid out of the booth. "Be right back," he said, patting her shoulder. "Just going to the men's room." He shuffled away.

Deirdre took a few bites of her sandwich. She started to feel a little calmer.

I'm actually out with Jon, she thought. I knew something good had to happen to me this year.

After a while she checked her watch. Where *was* Jon? How long had he been gone?

She glanced around the restaurant. No sign of him. "Weird."

She took another bite of the sandwich. Then she glanced around the restaurant again. Dana and Mickey had left.

She checked her watch. She drummed her fingers on the tabletop.

"Weird," she muttered again. She walked to the front window and peered out at the parking lot.

And let out a startled cry as she saw the empty parking spot. The empty space where Jon's car had been parked.

"Whoa—!" Deirdre spun around. And saw the two girl's laughing about something at Anita's table.

But Anita was gone, too.

Did Jon leave with Anita? Deirdre wondered, her heart pounding. Did he just dump me here and leave with her?

That is so cold, she told herself. How could he just leave me here?

Anita said she barely talks to him. So why would they leave together? Why would Jon sneak away like that?

Feeling miserable, feeling about as low as she ever had in her life, Deirdre paid the check. Then she trudged out of the restaurant.

I'm walking home again, she thought, sighing.

It's less than a mile. But here I am, walking

home alone for the second time tonight. . . .

The fog hadn't lifted at all. It actually seemed thicker, swallowing up the streetlights and swirling around like a damp, gray blanket.

Deirdre shivered and stuffed her hands in her pockets. Six or seven more blocks and I'll be home, she thought.

She picked up her pace.

A car sped by, music thundering from its windows. Its brake lights flared dimly as it turned the corner. Then the fog swallowed it up.

Deirdre stopped. What was that sound behind her?

A fluttering noise, like a bird's wings.

Deirdre spun around—and gasped as a figure stepped out from the gray fog.

A dark figure, sweeping toward her in a swirl of shadow. Surrounding her. Holding her.

Deirdre tried to scream, but the heavy shadow smothered her voice. The cold wrapped around her. Wrapped around her like a heavy blanket.

Can't breathe . . . Can't move . . .

She suddenly felt so weak.

Her knees began to buckle. She felt herself sinking.

Sinking into the blackness.

Sinking . . . sinking . . .

Her head slumped back. She felt cold, damp air on her face.

Hot breath on her neck.

And then, piercing pain. Like the stab of a knife at her throat.

Only darkness. Only silence.

Such a heavy silence.

And then a gentle lapping sound. A wet, lapping sound like a soft wave brushing a sandy shore.

Lap . . . Lap . . . Lap . . .

So soft and gentle and warm.

PART FIVE

Chapter Twenty-six

Thirst

have no choice.

I have to drink.

I am young and strong. I don't need to follow the old vampire rules.

I'm not afraid of sunlight.

I don't have to sleep in a coffin all day.

There is only one rule I must follow—I must drink!

Watching her in the restaurant, I knew she would quench my thirst. My terrible thirst . . .

But now—I am in trouble.

I almost had her. Her throat was bare. My teeth had just broken the skin.

I was about to nourish myself again.

A few sips. I had only a few sips.

And then . . . the car. Its music rumbled like

thunder. Its fog lights cut through the gray mist, lighting up the night.

Almost exposing me.

I had to run. I had to leave her there.

Deirdre.

Why did her twin have to arrive at that moment? I was so close. I had only a taste. I needed more . . .

More . . .

Dana and Deirdre. Do they know who I am?

Maybe.

So many rumors at the school. So many kids are suspicious.

I must finish both twins.

Then I will be strong again. But for now . . . I'm so thirsty!

I must drink.

Keep walking. Keep looking. I'll find someone.

I must.

What's that sound?

Something rustling on the sidewalk up ahead. Sniffing. Scratching.

A rabbit?

Yes.

Quiet. Move quietly.

One step. Another. Don't let it hear you.

There it is!

Ah—not a rabbit.

A dog.

A furry little Spaniel. Look at it pawing at that

greasy, wadded up food wrapper. Licking it. Trying to get a taste.

You're hungry, aren't you?

Your owner shouldn't have let you out alone.

Come here, doggie.

His fur so soft and warm . . . Let's turn you over. See your soft throat. Your soft belly.

Yes. Good dog. Good dog.

GOOD—DOGGGGGGGGG!

Don't squeal like that. It won't hurt for long.

Blood so warm, running down my chin.

Ohhhh . . . so gooood . . .

Chapter Twenty-seven

Another Accident

Deirdre jumped, gasping, as the final bell rang after school on Monday. Her knees felt rubbery as she left the room and headed for the gym.

Since Saturday night, every noise made her jump. Every sudden movement made her gasp. Every shadow made her heart pound and her hands shake.

I could be dead, she thought.

Dead . . .

If Dana and Mickey hadn't driven up, I would have been found lying in the street with every drop of blood drained from my body.

Drained dry . . . like the others.

Dana and Mickey didn't see anyone there except me.

The vampire killer escaped in time.

But he was there.

Holding me . . . murdering me.

Think about something else, Deirdre told herself. You're okay. You're safe now. Think about . . . Jon.

Jon?

She frowned.

She'd seen him in study hall. "I don't believe you! Why did you leave me there?" she demanded angrily. "Why did you leave me sitting there and go off with Anita?"

He stared at her as if he didn't recognize her. "I'm sorry," he murmured finally. "I don't understand what you're saying. I didn't leave with Anita. What makes you say that?"

"Well, why did you run out of the restaurant?" she asked shrilly.

"I felt sick," he explained. "I started to the men's room, and I suddenly felt sick. I mean, real sick. I had to get out of there. I called to you, Deirdre. I called and I waved. I thought for sure you heard me."

She studied his eyes, searching for the truth. "No. I didn't hear you," she replied finally. "And I didn't see you wave."

"I told you to get a ride with your sister," Jon continued. "And then I ran out. I—I felt so horrible. I was embarrassed, I guess. It was our first night out. I didn't want you to watch me hurling my guts out."

Do I believe him? Deirdre asked herself. The poor guy. Look how he's sweating.

"Well . . . I hope you're feeling better," she said. Kind of lame. But she didn't know what else to say.

"After you left . . ." she started. "I was walking home by myself and—"

The bell rang.

Deirdre glanced up at the wall clock. "Oh. I've got to run. A very important basketball practice." She grabbed his arm. "But I'd like to talk to you—"

"Me too," Jon replied. "Maybe we can drive to that cabin I told you about. You know. The one I fixed up in the woods. We could talk without being interrupted. There's a lot I'd like to tell you . . ." He hesitated.

"There's a lot you don't know about me," he blurted out. "About what happened at my old school. I feel I can trust you. I'd really like to talk to you."

His smile made her forget how frightened and upset she had been. She hurried to the gym—and bumped into Stacy.

Stacy had her hair in cornrows. Her team uniform was crisp and clean.

She greeted Deirdre coldly.

"Listen, I'm sorry I acted like a jerk Saturday," Deirdre said sincerely. "I really didn't mean to get into a fight."

"Me, either." Stacy's expression softened. She nudged Deirdre's shoulder. "Let's just forget about it."

"You look great," Deirdre told her. "I love your hair like that. It's totally awesome. How long did it take?"

"Only about ten hours!" Stacy laughed. "But I wanted to look super terrific for today. You know—because of the college recruiters who are coming."

"Where are they?"

Stacy pointed.

A man and a woman stood at one end of the gym, talking to Coach Martin. Both held clipboards and had serious, businesslike expressions on their faces.

"They don't look too excited to be at Shadyside High, do they?" Stacy said.

"No, but they haven't seen you play yet," Deirdre replied. "Wait till you go out on the floor. They won't look bored then."

"They better not. I've been waiting for this all my life!" Stacy exclaimed, squeezing Deirdre's wrist. "And I am *so* nervous. Feel my hand. It's ice cold."

"Don't worry, you'll be great," Deirdre assured her. "When they see you, they'll be dying to sign you up."

A piercing shriek from Coach Martin's whistle signaled the start of practice. The coach divided the team into two groups, then blew the whistle again to start a scrimmage.

Deirdre and Stacy were on the same team. Her friend played great, as usual—fast and strong and fearless.

So did Anita Black.

Anita was on the same team, but it didn't feel like it, Deirdre thought. When the two of them reached for the ball at the same time, Anita jabbed her elbow into Deirdre's ribs.

"Back off!" Deirdre warned.

"Sorry!" Anita cried. "It was an accident! I'm really sorry!"

Jennifer took a pass and quickly ducked away from her guard. Deirdre and Stacy both called for it. Jennifer shot the ball across the court.

They both went for the ball.

Stacy caught the pass.

She whirled around—and got tangled in Anita's legs.

Anita's foot tromped down on Stacy's.

Both girls fell hard. Anita landed on top of Stacy.

Deirdre pressed her hands against her face as Stacy let out a howl of pain.

"Sorry. Ohhh. I didn't mean—" Anita gasped, struggling to her feet. She rubbed her calf and bent down toward Stacy. "Are you okay?"

On her back, Stacy groaned in reply.

Anita reached down and pulled Stacy to her

feet. "I'm really sorry. Are you okay?" she repeated, pressing her hands against her cheeks.

Stacy tried to step down on her right foot.

But Deirdre could see the grimace of pain on her face.

Deirdre hurried over and put her arm around Stacy's waist.

Stacy's dark eyes blazed with anger as she stared at Anita. "What did you do that for?" she wailed. "Why didn't you watch where you were going?"

"I told you—it was an accident!" Anita screamed. A sob burst from her throat. She turned and ran off the floor, covering her face with her hands.

Stacy tried to put some weight on her foot, then sucked her breath in sharply. "Owww. It . . . really . . . hurts."

Coach Martin came running up. "Let's not take chances," she told Stacy. "Let's get you to a doctor."

"But the college recruiters—" Stacy started.

"Some other time," Coach Martin replied softly.

Deirdre drove Stacy to her doctor. The doctor took an X-ray. No broken bones. Just a bad bruise on the instep.

If Stacy rested the ankle for a week, the doctor said, she could be ready to play again.

"At least you'll only miss a few days of practice," Deirdre said as she slid behind the wheel of Stacy's car.

Stacy shot her an angry glance. "Don't try to give me a pep talk, Deirdre. You know how important today was. Those recruiters have probably already written me off. So excuse me if I don't celebrate!"

"I guess I did sound like some kind of cheerful idiot," Deirdre told her. "I'm sorry."

"No, I am." Stacy's eyes filled with tears. "I shouldn't yell at you. I'm just so upset. I don't know what to do!"

Deirdre started the car and pulled into the street. "I'll take you home so you can get your foot up."

"I don't want to go home!" Stacy wailed. "The first thing my parents will ask me is how it went. I can't stand to tell them—not yet."

Deirdre sighed and turned toward her house.

"I could kill Anita Black," Stacy muttered through gritted teeth. "Really. I could *kill* her."

"Please—don't say that," Deirdre begged her friend. "There have been two horrible murders already. And I . . . I came close . . ."

She stopped for a light and turned to her friend. "Please, don't talk about killing," Deirdre pleaded.

"I don't care," Stacy replied with a sob. "I don't care if it was an accident or not. I could kill Anita.

I could kill her easily. With my bare hands."

Deirdre didn't reply. The light changed. She lowered her foot to the gas, and they roared away.

The next afternoon Anita was found dead in the girls' shower room.

Chapter Twenty-eight

Caught!

The afternoon sun beamed down on the student parking lot, but Deirdre couldn't stop shivering. Her hands were icy, and her teeth chattered as if she stood in a freezing wind.

Small groups of kids had gathered outside Shadyside High. They talked in tense, worried murmurs and eyed the police cars parked in front of the school.

Dana and Stacy huddled close, hands jammed in their coat pockets. Dana shook her head glumly and kicked a pebble across the asphalt.

"I don't believe this," she whispered. "How can this be happening?"

"A policeman told me she was drained of blood, just like the others," Deirdre said. "I—I saw her face when they carried her out of the locker room. Her mouth was open, as if she'd been screaming. And her eyes . . . her eyes . . ."

Deirdre's voice cracked. She covered her face with her hands.

Dana wrapped her sister in a hug. They had to move out of the way as two more patrol cars rolled into the lot.

"I feel so horrible," Stacy murmured. "I mean, I said I wanted Anita dead, and now . . ."

"Don't feel guilty. Everybody says stuff like that sometimes," Dana told her. "You didn't kill her, Stacy. Words don't kill people." She leaned back against Mickey's car and shivered.

Dana is cold, too, Deirdre thought, gazing at her twin.

Except we're not really cold.

We're terrified.

"You know what I heard?" Dana said. "They might close the school for a while. They're going to have a big meeting about it tonight."

"Close it for how long?" Stacy asked.

Dana shrugged. "Until they catch the murderer, I guess."

"Maybe they should close it," Stacy said. "No one feels safe here. No one can think about school."

Deirdre shivered again.

Trisha's vision—it's really coming true, she thought.

Our class is doomed. We're dying, one by one—just as she predicted.

And who will be next?

"Deirdre—! Hey, Deirdre!"

She turned at the sound of her name. And saw Jon running across the parking lot, waving his arms excitedly, his dark hair blowing wild, his denim jacket open and flapping behind him.

"They've caught him!" Jon called breathlessly. "The police—they've caught the vampire!"

Chapter Twenty-nine

Another Shock

uh? They caught him?" Deirdre uttered a startled gasp.

The other girls cried out and rushed eagerly to Jon. A crowd of kids gathered around.

"Who was it?"

"Did they really catch someone?"

"Where is he? Are they bringing him out?"

"I don't see anyone. Are you sure it's true?"

"How did they catch him?"

Everyone had a million questions.

Jon struggled to catch his breath. He swept his hair off his forehead with one hand. And then pointed to the side exit of the school. "Look—! Over there!"

Deirdre turned and saw two grim-faced police

officers leading someone out of the building. He had his head bowed. His hands were cuffed behind him.

Even without seeing his face, Deirdre recognized him at once from his black clothing. Clark Dickson!

Count Clarkula.

"Clark really is the Vampire Killer?" she gasped.

Excited, startled murmurs rose from the crowd of kids.

Jon nodded.

"But how do they know he's the one?" Deirdre demanded.

"Jennifer Fear saw him running from the gym," Jon replied. "He couldn't explain why he was running."

"Oh, wow," Deirdre murmured, swallowing hard. "I don't believe it. Clark . . . Clark is a murderer. Clark is a . . . vampire!"

"We knew it all along," Dana said sadly. "If the police had only listened to us after Danielle's murder . . ."

"Two lives could have been saved," Stacy finished her thought for her.

"But how could Clark be so *sick*?" Dana cried. "How could someone we know get so *twisted*? How could he be a murderer?"

No one had an answer.

They watched the officers duck Clark's head as

they pushed him into the back seat of a patrol car.

Clark turned his head away so he wouldn't have to face the students gathered in the parking lot.

"This is such great news!" Jon declared, grabbing Deirdre's hands.

"It's over," Dana agreed, smiling for the first time. "The long nightmare—it's over."

"Maybe we can try to have a normal senior year now," Stacy sighed.

Jon tugged Deirdre's hands. "Come on. Let's go celebrate!"

Deirdre hesitated. "I don't know . . ."

"Come on!" Jon insisted. "Just the two of us!" He pulled her harder. "Remember that cabin I fixed up in the woods? It's such a beautiful day. I'm going there right now. Come with me—okay? I'll get some snacks. Some food and some Cokes, and we can—"

"Okay." Deirdre couldn't keep a smile from spreading across her face. "Sounds great! Let's go!"

Deirdre started to follow Jon. She stopped when she felt a hand on her arm.

"I don't mean to be a drip. But Mom said we should stick together and come right home," Dana reminded her.

"That was *before* they caught the murderer," Deirdre insisted. "I'll be home by dinnertime—right, Jon?"

Jon didn't have a chance to reply.

Mickey burst breathlessly into their group. "You . . . you're not going to . . . believe this!" he gasped. "It's so . . . *horrible*!"

Deirdre tugged her hands free and spun away from Jon.

"What is it?" she cried.

Chapter Thirty

A Surprise in the Cabin

"**A**nita's body—" Mickey announced. "It disappeared from the morgue!"

Deirdre uttered a sharp gasp.

"You mean—they *lost* it?" Jon cried.

Mickey shook his head. "The police said it just *disappeared*. Somebody *stole* it!"

Deirdre stared at Mickey, thinking hard, trying to figure out what this meant. Who would take Anita's body?

The murderer?

Another vampire?

Why would a vampire want her body if it was already drained of blood?

"I—I can't think straight," Deirdre blurted out, shaking her head hard, trying to clear it. "My thoughts are all a jumbled blur. Nothing I'm thinking makes any sense."

"Well . . . Clark didn't take the body," Stacy said thoughtfully. "We know that much. Clark was still here at school."

"But what does that *mean*?" Deirdre cried, tugging at her hair with both hands.

"Maybe Clark isn't the murderer," Dana said. "Maybe the real murderer is still out there. And maybe he stole Anita's body."

"Then it can't be anyone we know," Jon added. "Because everyone we know has been here at school."

He reached for Deirdre again. "Come on. I've got to get to the cabin. Let's get away from here! Before my head explodes."

Deirdre hesitated again. She glanced at Dana and caught a disapproving look.

"I—I'd better not," Deirdre told Jon. "Mom really insisted that Dana and I stick together and come home. And if the killer hasn't really been caught . . ." Her voice trailed off.

Jon sighed and tossed up his hands. "Okay. Some other time," he muttered.

"Some other time," Deirdre repeated.

Two hours later Deirdre and Dana made their way through the Fear Street Woods.

"This is totally crazy," Dana declared. "I can't believe I let you talk me into it."

"It's too late to quit now," Deirdre told her. "We're almost there. I think."

Deirdre paused and glanced around.

The sun hadn't set yet, but the woods had already grown dim and shadowy. The thick, tangled trees blocked out most of the light, even on the trail where Deirdre and Dana stood.

The air felt cold, and the trail was muddy from the weekend's rain. Wet leaves plastered the twins' sneakers.

"But why on earth are we doing this?" Dana demanded.

"You saw the disappointed look on Jon's face," Deirdre replied. "He really wanted to celebrate and show me his cabin."

"So why am I tagging along?" her twin asked, rolling her eyes.

"Because Mom told us to stick together. This way we can see the cabin and spend time with Jon. And I won't get into trouble."

They began following the trail again. "Almost there, I think," Deirdre repeated.

"What do you mean, you *think*?" Dana demanded.

"I know this is the trail Jon took that night when we found the cabin," Deirdre told her. "I'm just not sure how much longer we have to walk, that's all."

Dana moaned. Deirdre ignored her and plunged ahead.

The trail began to narrow until it almost disappeared in the soggy underbrush. Deirdre bent low to keep from running into any low-hanging branches. She slapped a mosquito on her arm.

We're getting very close, she thought.

She glanced over her shoulder to make sure Dana hadn't turned around and deserted her. Dana scowled at her, furiously brushing burrs from her hair. But she kept following.

"What if he isn't there?" Dana asked, peeling a wet leaf from her cheek.

"He *said* he was going to the cabin," Deirdre replied.

"Yeah, but . . ."

"There it is," Deirdre interrupted. She stopped and pointed.

The small cabin seemed even shabbier in the fading light. Dampness had turned the wooden slats dark gray, and Deirdre could see splotches of mossy-green rot on some of them.

"This is where Jon likes to hang out?" Dana asked skeptically. "In this broken-down little shack?"

"That's what he said," Deirdre replied. She could see her breath in the chilly air. "He found it one day. Deserted. And he fixed it up so he could get away and be by himself sometimes."

Dana rolled her eyes. "He can be by himself in this dump, that's for sure. Who would ever want to visit?"

Deirdre pushed through the weeds and underbrush and stopped at the cabin door. She knocked a couple of times and waited. "Hello!" she called. "Anybody in there?"

Silence.

"Weird," Deirdre murmured. "Jon? It's Dana and me! Are you in there?"

She tried the handle. It turned, but the door wouldn't open. She pushed with her shoulder.

"It won't budge," she declared. "The wood must be swollen from the rain or something."

"Let's get out of here, okay?" Dana asked. "I'm cold. And I'm getting a little freaked."

"Jon—?" Deirdre called. "Are you in there?" She turned back to her sister. "Let's see if there's a back door."

Dana laughed. "I'm surprised this place even has *one* door."

Dana was right. The cabin didn't have another door. But it did have a window on the back wall.

Deirdre tried to see inside, but years of grime clouded the old, rippled glass. She braced her hands on the warped frame and shoved.

The window stuck, then suddenly shot up with a piercing whine. Deirdre gasped and stumbled back against her sister.

"If Jon's here, he definitely heard that!" Dana exclaimed.

But no one shouted from inside the cabin. No one came to the window.

Deirdre crept to the window and peered inside.

"What's in there?" Dana whispered.

"I can't tell. It's too dark."

"Let's go," Dana insisted.

"He said he was coming here," Deirdre said. "Might as well take a look inside while we're here." She hoisted herself onto the window ledge.

Then she swung one leg over, stretching until her toe hit the floor. She ducked down and slid inside, dragging her other leg behind her.

"Help me in," Dana called.

Deirdre turned and helped pull her sister through the window. She brushed her hands off and peered around the dim room.

The fireplace took up one wall, its stones charred and blackened. A small heap of branches and sticks were piled on the floor next to it.

Cobwebs draped the walls and hung from the low ceiling.

Jon said he fixed it up, Deirdre thought. But he didn't even clean it! How could he possibly invite anyone in here? How could he even stand it himself?

No rug on the dusty floor. Not a single chair or even a cushion to sit on.

The room held only one piece of furniture. A black, hulking mass that blocked the door.

Huh? That's what kept us from getting in, Deirdre realized.

What is it?

The Thirst

Deirdre walked across the room and stopped, staring in horror.

A long, black box stood in front of the door. A long, waist-high box with a rusty brass handle on one side.

A coffin.

Chapter Thirty-one

The Vampire Awakens

Gaping at the long, black coffin, Deirdre began to shake all over.

What is this doing here?

Is this the vampire's cabin?

Is someone inside this coffin?

She heard footsteps, close behind her.

Deirdre screamed and spun around.

"Deirdre, it's just me!" Dana cried. "What is it? What's that box?"

Deirdre tried to answer, but no sound came out. She swallowed hard. Cleared her throat. Tried again. "We have to get out of here! We have to find the police!"

Dana grabbed hold of Deirdre's shoulder. She stared at the coffin. "Is it . . . Jon's?" she asked in a whisper. "Is Jon the vampire?"

"No. He can't be!" Deirdre cried. "He must not know the coffin is here. Or maybe . . ." She didn't know what to think.

If Jon was the vampire, did he invite her to the cabin to drink her blood? To murder her?

Was she supposed to be the next victim?

No. No way.

Jon was too nice. Too normal.

No way Jon could be a vampire.

But then, how do I explain the coffin in front of the door?

Jon said he was coming here. Was he asleep inside the coffin right now?

Or were they in the *wrong* cabin? Deirdre had seen the cabin late at night, covered in darkness.

Had she led them to the wrong place? Had they stumbled onto the vampire's cabin by mistake?

"L-let's go," she stammered. She grabbed Dana's hand and they raced toward the window.

"Wait!" Dana clutched Deirdre's arm, holding her back. "Did you hear that?"

Deirdre heard the snap of a twig outside. Branches rustled. Another twig snapped.

"Someone's coming!" Dana whispered. "Coming toward the window. If it's Jon . . ."

The twins whirled around. Could we squeeze out the door? Deirdre wondered.

They were almost to the coffin when a creaking sound made them both gasp in fright.

"Ohhhh." Deirdre uttered a terrified moan as

she saw the coffin lid begin to lift.

She froze. She felt Dana tugging at her. But she couldn't move.

Creak ... creak ...

The lid lifted slowly at first. And then it suddenly flew wide open, slamming hard against the cabin door.

The door shuddered. Cobwebs swayed, and a cloud of dust swirled through the air.

A pale hand appeared. Long, slender fingers grasped the edge of the coffin.

The vampire sat up quickly. Blinked a few times. Stared at the two sisters.

And then leaped from the coffin, ready to attack.

Chapter Thirty-two

Too Late for Deirdre

"**A**nita!" Deirdre shrieked, staring in disbelief.

Dana grabbed Deirdre's arm, too stunned to make a sound.

Anita's dark red hair tumbled to her shoulders in shiny waves. Her skin was still pale, but her lips were bright red.

And her green eyes glowed with life.

"You figured it out, didn't you?" Anita asked, slowly circling her way around the twins. "That's why you're here. You figured it out."

"But . . . but you're *dead*!" Deirdre gasped. "Your blood was drained!"

"Yes. It was drained fifty years ago, when I became a vampire." Anita sighed. A tired, bitter smile crossed her face. "It's really easy for me to play dead."

Dana whimpered and dug her fingers into Deirdre's arm.

Anita laughed suddenly, tossing her head back. "What's the matter—did you expect me to look like Count Dracula? Things have changed, girls. I don't hide from the sun. I don't need to sleep in coffins. I don't even *like* them, but this one came in handy. You see, I needed a place to hide for a while."

Anita stopped circling and stood with her back to the window. "I thought I'd fooled you, but you figured it out. I knew that one of you saw me that morning in the gym, when I was finishing the first one—what was her name?"

"Danielle," Dana answered in a murmur, her voice shaking.

"Yes. Danielle." Anita shut her eyes and smiled. She licked her lips, as if she could still taste Danielle's blood.

"But I *didn't* see you!" Dana protested. "I never knew it was you!"

Anita frowned. "I shouldn't have done it in school where I'd be seen. But I was so thirsty! I couldn't control myself. I thought one of you saw me. So I tried to take care of you on the overnight camping trip. But you started to wake up. I only got a taste."

Deirdre shuddered.

"Anyway, I had another reason to go after you by then," Anita continued. "Except you look so much alike, I got the wrong one."

Unconsciously Deirdre reached up and touched the mole on her cheek. It's me she was after! Not Dana . . .

Anita stared at her. "Yes, you. Deirdre. You're the one I really wanted."

"But . . . why?" Deirdre choked out.

Anita's green eyes narrowed menacingly. "You stole someone from me."

"What—what are you talking about?" Deirdre stammered.

"Jon was mine—until he met you."

"I—I don't understand," Deirdre whispered.

The vampire moved closer.

"The minute he met you, he started to break away from me. I wanted to kill him, but . . . I love him. So I had to get rid of you. At first I just tried to scare you off. Too bad you didn't pay any attention to my messages."

The phone calls, Deirdre thought. The note. Shoving me into the fire. Going after me in basketball.

"But it's too late now," Anita declared. "Jon will be mine again, once I'm finished." She turned to Dana. "It's too bad you let your sister bring you here. Too bad . . . I can't let either one of you leave, you know."

She stepped toward them.

Deirdre screamed and backed away, pulling Dana with her.

Anita advanced on them, her eyes flashing.

Deirdre gazed desperately around the room. The only way out is through the window! she realized. And we can't get to it!

The twins backed up against the coffin. The lid slammed down.

Deirdre screamed in terror.

Grabbing Dana's hand, she tried to run. But her foot caught on the pile of firewood. Branches and sticks scattered across the floor.

She felt Dana stumble behind her. Dana screamed, and Deirdre lost hold of her hand.

She whirled around.

Dana lay sprawled face down on the floor on her stomach.

Deirdre reached for her sister.

But Anita clamped a hand around Deirdre's wrist and dragged her away.

"It's too late!" Anita cried, spinning Deirdre around to face her. "Too late. Too late . . ."

Deirdre struggled, but Anita was too strong. She grabbed hold of Deirdre's hair and yanked her head back, exposing her throat.

Deirdre felt cold air flowing across her skin.

She struggled frantically, but she couldn't break free.

"Nooooo!" she uttered a howl of protest.

Anita's face loomed close.

Her mouth opened.

Her sharp fangs slid down.

"Nooooooo!" Another terrified howl burst from

Deirdre's throat.

Anita's eyes gleamed above her.

Too strong. She's too strong, Deirdre realized.

With a hungry smile, lips dripping with saliva, Anita lowered her head to Deirdre's throat.

Chapter Thirty-three

The Vampire Must Die!

No, please. No.

Her eyes on the vampire, Dana scrambled to her feet. Dust stung her eyes and clogged her throat. Choking, she squinted through a film of tears.

"Nooo! Please—no!"

Anita was lowering her fangs toward the smooth, taut skin of Deirdre's throat.

"Anita, nooo!"

Dana lurched toward the vampire.

As she dived forward, she caught a flash of movement.

A figure, moving quickly through the open window.

Jon!

Jon landed in a crouch, a terrified expression twisting his face.

"No!" he shouted at Anita, his voice booming through the small cabin. "I'm warning you, Anita! Let go of her! Now!"

Anita ignored him. Her eyes flashed. Saliva rolled down her chin.

With a wild cry of anticipation, she snapped her head down to Deirdre's throat.

Dana opened her mouth in a scream and stumbled toward her sister.

Jon shoved her aside.

Startled, Dana staggered sideways and crashed into the wall. Her head slammed hard against the wood. Tiny black dots danced in front of her eyes.

"Let her go, Anita!" Jon insisted. "Listen to me! You can't do this!"

Dana shook her head. Her vision began to clear.

She pushed away from the wall.

And stopped in shock.

She watched Jon pick up one of the firewood branches from the floor. About two feet long and an inch around, the branch tapered to a point at one end.

Dana couldn't take her eyes off that point.

Couldn't blink.

Couldn't breathe . . .

Jon lunged at Anita. He grabbed her shoulder and spun her around.

Deirdre collapsed to the floor.

With a ferocious bellow of anger, Jon rammed

the pointed end of the branch—rammed it deep into Anita's chest.

Anita froze. Her eyes bulged in shock.

She sucked in her breath.

Her hideous, rattling gasp of pain seemed to shake the cabin.

Screaming in horror, Dana raced to her sister. "Deirdre, are you all right? Deirdre? Deirdre?"

She knelt down, gripping Deirdre's shoulders and pulling her into a sitting position. "Deirdre!"

Deirdre groaned and raised her fingers to her throat.

Dana pushed her sister's hand away and peered closely. Nothing. No bite marks. "You're okay!" she cried in relief. "Jon stopped her in time!"

Deirdre began to shake. As Dana wrapped her arms around her, another rattling breath rose up from Anita.

Clinging to her sister, Dana gaped at the dying vampire.

Anita was moving now, staggering around in a small circle. Her fingers scrabbled at the length of wood poking out from her chest.

"Idiot!" she cried bitterly, seething at Jon. Thick saliva dripped from her fangs and rolled down her chin. "What have you done?"

Jon didn't reply.

"What have you . . ." Anita's eyes suddenly filled with terror. Her body began to tremble, and she fell back to the floor.

A piercing, shrill cry rose from her mouth.

Dana cringed, shuddering at the sound. The vampire's shriek rose higher and higher, filling the room like a siren.

Anita's body trembled harder.

And then her arms began to shrivel.

Dana gasped in horror as she watched Anita's body shrivel and shrink. The skin wrinkled and puckered, began to flake off.

Her hair lost its color, then crumbled into soft, tiny shreds that vanished into the dust on the floor.

Anita is disintegrating! Dana realized.

The piercing shriek faded slowly. Faded to a hiss of wind.

Anita's face crumpled in on itself. The pale skin fell off, flaked, sifted onto the floor.

Silence now.

Anita's green eyes flashed, then grew dull and lifeless.

Her skull cracked open. Her bones broke and cracked.

The pointed branch toppled to the floor with a soft thud. Bounced once. Then lay still.

Dana stared down at a fine, gray powder. Powder. Just powder. All that was left of Anita.

A cold draft of air blew in through the window.

The dust and powder sifted together into a tiny whirlwind that spun into the fireplace and rose up through the chimney.

Silence. Silence.

It's over, Dana thought. The vampire is dead, forever.

Jon took a deep breath. "Are you okay?" he asked Dana.

"*I* am. Thank goodness you got here!" Dana tightened her arms around her sister. "Deirdre, are you all right?"

"I—I think so," Deirdre murmured shakily. "I was so scared! And the way she died—it was so horrible!"

"I know, but we're all okay." Dana helped Deirdre to her feet. "Thanks, Jon. You saved our lives."

"Yeah, well . . ." Jon shrugged, an embarrassed expression on his face. "Don't think I wasn't scared, too. But you're right—it's over. We won't have to be afraid anymore. No one will. No more murders. No more ugly phone calls. We can all relax now, and—"

"Nooooo!"

A long, low cry burst from Deirdre's throat.

She jerked away from Dana.

Flew across the room—and snatched the tree branch from the floor.

Then, with another fierce cry, Deirdre whirled around—and stabbed the pointed end deep into Jon's chest.

Jon went rigid.

The Thirst

His mouth gaped open, but no sound came out. His pale eyes bulged in shock.

Dana grabbed her sister by the shoulders and pulled her back. "Are you crazy?" Dana shrieked. "Are you *crazy*?"

Chapter Thirty-four

Even More Horror?

Deirdre staggered back from Jon. Her knees shook so badly she nearly collapsed to the cabin floor.

"I killed him," she murmured. "I killed Jon . . ."

"Are you *crazy*?" Dana shrieked again. "He—he saved our lives!"

"I know," Deirdre replied in a whisper. "I know what he did."

"Then why . . ."

Dana broke off with a gasp as a sharp sound interrupted her.

A wailing, siren-like shriek coming from Jon's mouth.

Deirdre shivered and wrapped her arms around herself. She didn't want to watch, but she couldn't make herself look away.

I have to see it.

I have to make sure.

Jon trembled violently, then slumped to the floor.

His arms and legs began to shrink. His skin shriveled and flaked, turned to powder. His eyes melted into their sockets. His mouth opened in a skeletal grin, and his teeth tumbled out, sprinkling over the floor.

Gray skull bone poked through his forehead. His head tilted forward, and his eyeballs dropped onto the floor at Deirdre's feet.

His bones broke apart, crumbling into smaller and smaller pieces. Crumbling . . . crumbling . . . until nothing remained but a fine, gray dust.

Silence now.

Such a deep, heavy silence.

He's gone, Deirdre thought. Gone for good.

She turned to Dana.

"Jon was a vampire, too," Deirdre murmured, staring in shock at the wooden stake, lying in the thin layer of dust on the floor.

"How did you know, Deirdre? How did you know?" her sister asked in a whisper.

"The phone calls," Deirdre replied. "He said that with Anita dead, there wouldn't be any more ugly phone calls."

Dana shrugged, a confused expression on her face. "So?"

"I never told him about the calls," Deirdre said. "I never mentioned them to him. I never told anyone but you."

"But if Anita told him about the calls—?" Dana started.

"No," Deirdre replied softly, shaking her head. "He wasn't at all surprised to see the coffin. And he wasn't surprised to find a vampire in his cabin. He tried to fool us by killing her. But you heard what Anita said. Jon was hers. They were a couple. They belonged together. Think about it, Dana. How can you belong to a vampire and not *be* one?"

Dana shuddered.

Deirdre stared down at the powdery dust scattered across the floor. She rubbed the toe of her shoe in it.

Dust. Just dust.

Then she took her sister's arm and led her out of the cabin.

"This way," Deirdre said, pointing. "The cabin is down this path."

Beams of yellow light from their flashlights darted over the dew-wet ground, dancing over the trees and shrubs.

The two Shadyside police officers followed Deirdre and Dana, grumbling about the damp cold night.

"There it is," Dana announced, shining her light on the cabin.

Gazing at the shabby little place, Deirdre

couldn't help feeling a chill of fear.

But it's empty, she reminded herself.

The vampires are gone. They're never coming back.

The police hurried to the cabin door.

"You can't get in that way," Deirdre told them. "It's blocked off. There's a big coffin blocking the door. You can't—"

Deirdre broke off as the door swung open and banged against the inside wall. She clutched Dana's arm. "Hey—! The coffin! I don't believe it! What *happened* to it?"

The officers aimed their flashlights through the doorway.

A huge cloud of dust had risen into the air. It swirled in the twin beams of light, then gradually began to settle.

"It's gone," Deirdre murmured, stunned. "It must have disintegrated, too."

The police stepped into the doorway, sweeping their lights all around the room. Dana and Deirdre peered in behind them.

Branches and sticks lay scattered across the floor. The pointed branch lay in the center of the cabin, exactly where it had fallen when Jon died.

No trace of the vampires or their coffin. No trace . . .

The officers stepped outside and pulled the door shut. They glanced at each other, then at the twins.

"I know what you're thinking, but you're

wrong," Deirdre told them. "We're not lying. We didn't make this up."

"Nobody is accusing you of lying," the policeman said.

"Well, we're not crazy, either," Dana insisted.

"Of course you're not." The second officer patted Dana's shoulder sympathetically. "Don't feel bad," he told her. "Everyone in town is scared. Everyone's imagination is running wild."

Shaking their heads, the two officers led the way back along the trail.

"They think we're hysterical idiots," Deirdre muttered as Dana drove them home.

"Who cares?" Dana replied. "We know we didn't imagine it. We know it really happened. And it's over." She sighed. "The horror is over."

Dana pulled the car into the driveway and shut the engine off. She and Deirdre climbed out and walked up the front steps.

They both gasped as a figure moved quickly from the shadows at the side of the house. Squinting into the dim porch light, Deirdre recognized Trisha Conrad.

"Trisha? What is it?" Deirdre cried. "What's wrong?"

Trisha lurched up to them breathlessly, her blond hair wild about her face, her eyes wide with horror. "I just had another *horrible* vision about you two!" she cried. "You won't *believe* what I just saw!"

"You're right," Deirdre replied. "We *won't* believe it."

She and Dana hurried into the house and slammed the door behind them.

R.L. Stine
Seniors
a FEAR STREET series

available from Gold Key® Paperbacks

FEAR STREET® titles
available from Gold Key® Paperbacks:

The Stepbrother
Camp Out
Scream, Jennifer, Scream!
The Bad Girl

FEAR STREET® **Sagas**
available from Gold Key® Paperbacks:

Circle of Fire
Chamber of Fear
Faces of Terror
One Last Kiss

About R.L. Stine

R.L. Stine is the best-selling author in America. He has written more than one hundred scary books for young people, all of them bestsellers.

His series include *Fear Street, Ghosts of Fear Street,* and the *Fear Street Sagas*.

Bob grew up in Columbus, Ohio. Today he lives in New York City with his wife, Jane, his son, Matt, and his dog, Nadine.

Don't Miss
FEAR STREET® Seniors
Episode Four!

NO ANSWER

Her dead sister, Justine, really *did* contact her through
a psychic hotline——and Clarissa discovers her sister's
death was not an accident——it was murder.

Now Clarissa realizes that another Shadyside senior is
about to die.

And it could be her!